Books by Janwillem van de Wetering

The Empty Mirror
A Glimpse of Nothingness
Outsider in Amsterdam
Tumbleweed

Published by POCKET BOOKS

TUMBLEWEED

Janwillem van de Wetering

A KANGAROO BOOK
PUBLISHED BY POCKET BOOKS NEW YORK

POCKET BOOKS, a Simon & Schuster division of
GULF & WESTERN CORPORATION
1230 Avenue of the Americas, New York, N.Y. 10020

Published by arrangement with Houghton Mifflin Company
Library of Congress Catalog Card Number: 76-1865

ISBN: 0-671-81339-0

First Pocket Books printing April, 1978

Trademarks registered in the United States and other countries.

Printed in the U.S.A.

for Anne Barrett

TUMBLEWEED

1

ADJUTANT-DETECTIVE GRIJPSTRA felt that this was not the best morning of the year. He sat slouched behind his gray steel desk in the large room in Headquarters that he shared with his assistant, Detective-Sergeant de Gier, and held his heavy square head between his hands. He was studying the Telex reports of the previous day, printed on cheap pink paper and filed in a worn loose-leaf ledger. His head ached and his throat felt parched and hurt whenever he tried to swallow, which was often.

"Have you noticed," he asked hoarsely, "that nothing ever happens in Amsterdam?"

He was asking himself, and his voice was very low. The heavy early-morning traffic in Marnix Street should have drowned his question but two cars which had collided two blocks down were obstructing all traffic and de Gier had heard him.

"Should be in bed," de Gier thought, and asked "Hmm?" in a loud voice because he didn't want to leave his superior unprotected in his loneliness.

"In Amsterdam," Grijpstra repeated, "nothing ever happens."

"You are ill," de Gier said, "you have flu. Go home and go to bed. Take aspirins and drink tea. Tea and brandy, and lemon, in a glass. Nice and hot. After that, sleep. Sleep all day. Tomorrow you can read the paper. Day after tomorrow you can read a book. Day after that another book. Day after that is Saturday. Day after that is Sunday. Go for a walk. Come back on Monday."

"Nothing the matter with me," Grijpstra said in a muffled voice, and lit a cigarette. He coughed a few times, went into a fit of coughing, and nearly choked.

De Gier smiled and continued to think. "No wonder he doesn't want to go home. Two floors in a narrow house at the Lijnbaansgracht isn't much space. And there is already Mrs. Grijpstra to fill that space, and the three little Grijpstras, and the TV."

Grijpstra also thought. His thoughts were negative, irritable, spiteful. "Look at him," Grijpstra thought. "Handsome fellow, isn't he? Lovely suit he is wearing. Dark blue denim, tailor made. Pale blue shirt. And that little scarf. Dandy! And the curly hair! And that nose. Bloody film star. Bah."

But Grijpstra corrected himself. He told himself not to be jealous. He reminded himself that de Gier was his friend. A loyal modest friend. He forced himself to remember the two occasions that de Gier had risked his life for him. He forced himself to forget the three occasions on which he had risked his own life to save de Gier's. "We are in Amsterdam," he told himself. "In Amsterdam the crooks threaten, but they don't kill. It's an easy town. Nothing ever happens in Amsterdam."

He had said it aloud again, and de Gier bent down to read the pink Telex reports.

"What do you mean?" de Gier asked. "Look at this. Plenty happens."

He was standing next to the set of drums which had

once, long ago now, miraculously appeared in their room and which Grijpstra had refused to return to whoever might own it. Grijpstra used the drums in his empty moments to revive the dreams of his youth when he had planned to become a jazz musician; and de Gier, at times, accompanied him on a small flute, a relic from de Gier's early days when he played church music at the Dutch Reformed School.

De Gier picked up one of the drumsticks. "Plenty happens. Here. Traffic accidents (bam on the drum), stolen bicycles (bam) car slipped into the canal (bam.)" Grijpstra groaned at the bams. "And here! (roll on the drum) Armed robbery. Three men holding up old lady in cigar store. Lady wounded. That's real crime. Attempted manslaughter, that should have been ours."

"Not ours," Grijpstra said. "Sietsema and Geurts are taking care of that."

"Sietsema is a motor cop," de Gier said.

"He was transferred to the crime squad. Fell off his Guzzi once too often, didn't you hear?"

De Gier put down his drumsticks and looked out of the window. The traffic was moving again and growled past Headquarters, farting its fumes into open windows where policemen were getting ready to deal with another day of maintaining lawful order. De Gier once wanted to be a motor cop but had allowed himself to be talked into detection. "You have a good brain, de Gier," the staff officer had told him, "don't waste your good brain, de Gier." He always wondered if the choice had been right. He could have been a sergeant on a motorcycle, same pay, same conditions. A large white shining Guzzi. Motor cops don't have flat feet. Neither had de Gier, but he would one day. Detectives walk too much. They wait at street corners. They climb endless stairs, usually the wrong stairs. Motor cops never climb stairs.

"Maybe Sietsema and Geurts will make a mess of it, and the chief inspector will give the job to us."

"He won't," Grijpstra said, and sneezed.

"Shall I get you a nice cup of coffee?"

"Yes," Grijpstra said.

De Gier went to the door, opened it, and froze.

"Gentlemen," the commissaris said.

The commissaris smiled. The time that noncommissioned officers jumped to attention at the mere sight of a passing commissaris was long past. Soon he wouldn't be even called "sir." But some of the men still remembered the old days and showed their memory.

"Sir," some of these men were saying now.

"I was just going out to get some coffee. Can I get you a cup?"

"Please," the commissaris said.

"A cigar, sir?" Grijpstra asked, opening the drawer where he kept the tin of little cigars the commissaris liked.

"Please," the commissaris said.

"Sit down, sir," Grijpstra said, and pointed at the only comfortable chair the room owned.

The commissaris sat down, stroking his left leg, which had kept him awake some of the night. Grijpstra noticed the movement of the hand and wondered how long the little old man would wander around the large Headquarters building. He still had five service years to go but his rheumatism seemed to be getting worse lately. Much worse. Twice Grijpstra had seen the commissaris leaning against a wall, paralyzed with pain, his face a white horrible mask.

De Gier had come back with a plastic tray holding three paper cups. The commissaris took a careful sip, and looked at his two detectives.

"You remember the houseboat on the Schinkel?" the commissaris asked.

"The one the chief inspector asked us to keep an eye on?" Grijpstra asked.

"Right," the commissaris said. "The chief inspector is

on holiday now and I don't know how much he has told you. What do you know?''

Grijpstra grinned. ''Not much, sir. The chief inspector never tells us very much. All we know is that we should keep an eye open.''

''Have you?''

Grijpstra looked at de Gier.

De Gier took his cue. ''We pass that boat at least twice a week, sir, and we have reported to the chief inspector. I have been there by myself as well, on my bicycle and once or twice at night, on foot. It's a nice walk from where I live and it's spring now, I like going there. But there isn't much to tell. The houseboat is expensive, and has two stories. There is only one occupant, a thirty-four-year-old woman. Her name is Maria van Buren, born on the island of Curaçao. She is a divorcee and is still using her husband's name. He is a director of a textile factory in the North.''

''Tell us about the woman,'' the commissaris said.

''A beautiful woman,'' de Gier said. ''Not altogether white. She drives a white Mercedes sports car, five years old but in good repair. At least three men visit her and stay the night or part of the night. I have the numbers of their cars.''

''You know who the men are?''

De Gier nodded. ''One man is a Belgian diplomat, stationed in The Hague. Drives a black Citroën. He is forty-five years old, looks like a tennis player. The second man is an American army officer, a colonel, stationed in Germany. The third is Dutch, a tall man going bald, fifty-eight years old. I checked him out and he is a big shot, chairman of several companies. He has a house in town but his family lives on Schiermonnikoog* or rather his

*An island in the North of Holland, 18 square miles, population 900.

wife does for his children are grown up. His name is
IJsbrand Drachtsma.''

"Did you come to any conclusions?''

De Gier looked noncommittal. "No, sir.''

The commissaris looked at Grijpstra.

"Could be just a woman who likes a bit of company,''
Grijpstra said, "could be that she is earning a little pocket
money on the side. We investigated the Dutchman,
IJsbrand Drachtsma. He seems a solid citizen. Very
wealthy, very respectable. A tycoon in business. The
companies he works for do very well. Chemicals, textiles,
building materials. A hero as well. He escaped to England
during the second year of the war, when the Germans were
watching the beaches. In a rowboat, I believe, with three
others. They had a small engine but it broke down. Joined
the British army and came back fighting, through France
and Belgium.''

"Did you find out anything about the other two?''

"No, sir,'' Grijpstra said, "but I am sure the chief
inspector did. We gave him all the details and he seemed
interested.''

"Did you make any inquiries about the woman?''

"No,'' Grijpstra said. "We checked with the municipal
files but that was all. We were told to be discreet so we
didn't ask about. We could, of course. There are some
other boats nearby.''

"Anything special about that woman, sir?'' de Gier
asked, trying not to show any excitement.

"Yes,'' the commissaris said. "You know that we have
a Secret Service.'' He smiled and the two detectives
guffawed. They were aware of the existence of the Secret
Service. It occupied two rooms on the floor above them,
rooms filled with a few middle-aged men and aged secretaries. The middle-aged men talked a lot of football and
the secretaries were always typing. Poems, according to
Grijpstra. Bad poems. Grijpstra claimed that Holland has
no secrets and that the Secret Service was only formed to

fill a gap in the state's budget. But the Secret Service was a larger organization than whatever went on in the two rooms above them. They occupied other offices as well, in The Hague and in Rotterdam. They were linked with several ministries, with mayors and with chief constables. They were even linked with the crown, the supreme mystery of the democracy. They might, Grijpstra had once whispered, be connected with God, the Dutch God, an old man living in a stuffy room, a powerful manifestation wearing slippers and interested in a wide range of phenomena, such as waterworks, the price of butter, theology, the right to argue, and Ajax, the national soccer team.

"The Secret Service," Grijpstra repeated, doing his best to look serious.

"Yes," the commissaris said, "they are interested in Mrs. van Buren and they asked us to keep an eye on her. For some reason they don't seem to have their own detectives. The tax department has, and the customs have and the army has, but they haven't. They like to use us. When was the last time that you had a look at the houseboat?"

"Today is Tuesday," de Gier said. "I was there on Thursday. I meant to go during the weekend but I had a friend staying with me. Do you know why the Secret Service is interested, sir?"

"No," the commissaris said, "but we may find out. Something seems to be wrong. We had a telephone call from the man staying in the boat next door to hers. He says he hasn't seen her for a few days and he wants us to come and have a look. Her cat is wandering about the area and wants to move in with him. He has rung her bell but she doesn't open the door. Her car is parked in front of the boat."

"When did the call come in, sir?" Grijpstra asked.

"Just now. Quarter of an hour ago. I want you to go there and break in if necessary. I brought a warrant."

"Don't you want to come with us, sir?" de Gier asked.

"No. I have a meeting with the chief constable. If there is anything wrong you can reach me via your radio or the telephone." The commissaris rubbed his leg, got up with some difficulty, and walked out of the room, trying not to limp.

Within a few minutes they were in Marnix Street waiting at a traffic light. A small motorcycle ignored the red light and raced past a truck coming from the right, managing to miss it.

"No," de Gier said, but it had happened already. The motorcycle missed the truck, it even missed another truck, but then the rider lost control and the cycle went into a spin. When the helmet of the young man crashed against the sidewalk Grijpstra reached for the microphone.

"Corner of Marnix Street and Passeerders Street. Motorcycle. Please call an ambulance. Detectives de Gier and Grijpstra witnesses but no time to stop. Over."

"O.K. Out," the voice from Headquarters answered.

A little later they heard the sirens. De Gier made way for the ambulance and, within seconds, for a white police Volkswagen. Both had their blue lights flashing.

"You think he is dead?" de Gier asked.

Grijpstra shrugged. "Perhaps his helmet saved him, but he must be badly hurt. Crushed his shoulder maybe and his leg. A hot engine burns through your leg in no time at all. He may never walk properly again."

De Gier drove calmly, trying to forget the accident and concentrating on what he remembered about the houseboat.

Even with all the lights against them it didn't take long. A short bearded man was standing near the houseboat's door.

"Police," Grijpstra said as he got out of the car. "Are you the one who phoned?"

"I am," the man said. "Bart de Jong is the name. Call me Bart, everybody does. I live in that boat over there."

Grijpstra shook the man's hand and said his name. De Gier joined them. Bart looked unusual, but not very unusual, considering they were in Amsterdam. A short-set strong-looking man some forty years old. The beard seemed to grow right up to his small twinkly eyes. Dark eyes, like beads, black and pearly. The left ear was decorated with a gold earring. He wore a corduroy suit and an open-necked shirt and leather boots, beautifully polished, covering his ankles. The narrow trouser legs had been tucked into the boots. The man looked clean, even his hair was neatly brushed.

"What's this about the lady's cat?" Grijpstra asked.

Bart offered cigarettes. De Gier noticed that his hand shook as he held the burning match. "Ah. The cat. The cat has been bothering me for the last two days. The cat often calls on me, scratches my door and I let him in. Beautiful animal, a Persian. There he is now."

A cat came stalking along the narrow path leading to a small houseboat, lying next to the luxurious structure that was directly facing them. De Gier squatted down and patted the cat's head while it rubbed itself against his leg, half-closing the large yellow luminous eyes in obvious pleasure.

"Friendly animal," de Gier said. "I prefer Siamese cats myself but this one is pretty, has a lot of fur."

"Exactly," Bart said, "that's what I've got against him. I don't mind him visiting me and he can get milk and meat any time he likes but he wants much more. He is used to being properly pampered, hair has got to be brushed ten times a day for he doesn't like things sticking to it, and he walks through the plants here and messes himself up. And if you refuse to brush him he begins to whine and scratch your legs. If he does that I send him home, but he has kept on coming back for the last two days. I rang Mrs. van Buren's bell but she doesn't want to open her door. Her car is here and I am sure she is home, so perhaps something happened to her.''

"Let's try the bell again," de Gier said.

They rang the bell, knocked and shouted. No response.

"So?" Bart asked.

"We'll break the door."

"I thought even the police weren't allowed to break doors in this country," Bart said.

"We are special police," de Gier said, "and we have a warrant."

"And we won't break the door," Grijpstra said. "Let's find another way."

De Gier reached out from the gangway and studied a window.

"You have long legs," Grijpstra said.

De Gier nodded and produced his pistol. The glass broke with the first tap of its butt.

"Careful now," Grijpstra said. "Last time you climbed through a window you hurt yourself and bled all over your suit."

"I live and learn," de Gier said, and eased his arm through the broken window. The window swung open after a while and de Gier, supported by Grijpstra, climbed through. Within seconds the front door opened.

"You don't want me to come in?" Bart asked.

"No. Wait here. We won't be long. Hell! Watch it."

The cat, which had been with them on the boat's gangplank and had seemed to be eager to get in, had suddenly made an extraordinary sound, a deep yowl ending in a blood-curdling shriek, and had turned in a flash and rushed off. It stopped at a safe distance and sat down. Its thick furry coat seemed twice its usual size.

Bart was shaking his head. "That's not so good. You better go in and see what's wrong. Something is wrong."

"Yes," Grijpstra said, and pushed his body into movement. He tapped de Gier on the shoulder. De Gier was still watching the cat.

They found nothing in the lower story of the boat. Everything looked in order, a bit dusty possibly. The lady had decorated her home with a strange taste. A strange but expensive taste. Persian carpets, a large stone fireplace. De Gier stopped a second in front of a statue carved out of wood, depicting three female figures standing on top of one another. Their breasts were exaggerated, pointed, with long nipples. The lips were thick and the foreheads low. The three tongues, lolling in three open mouths, had been painted red, and the very white teeth were pointed seashells. An African fertility symbol perhaps, he thought, but there was more than fertility in the three figures. They seemed to radiate some strong power.

There were other statues in the room. On a shelf he saw at least a dozen little men, varying in height from two to six inches. They were African warriors, carrying spears and other weapons. All the little men looked very intent, as if their ferocity was directed at a common goal.

"Me," de Gier thought, "they want me. What the hell do they want me for?"

But he felt comforted immediately. They didn't want just him, they would want anyone who came in their way.

"Nice place," said Grijpstra, who had gone to the next room.

"You think so?" de Gier asked politely.

"Yes," Grijpstra said, looking about him. "Lots of space. Nice comfortable chairs. A man could sit here and read his paper or one of those books and smoke a cigar. Very pleasant. Look at that painting."

De Gier looked. The painting was peaceful, dreamy. A Pierrot and his Columbine strolling through a garden lit by the moon, a pale dark garden. The background of the scene was formed by a line of poplars, bare poplars, so it would be winter. There were some strangely shaped clouds in the metallic blue sky, small clouds with sharp white edges.

"You like that painting?" de Gier asked.

"Yes," Grijpstra said, "much better than all that pink flesh you see nowadays. It's very sexy but they are fully clothed. They aren't even holding hands you see, just arm in arm, respectable, pleasant."

"They must have made love to each other in that little summerhouse next to the poplars," de Gier said.

Grijpstra looked at the summerhouse. "Yes," he said slowly. "That's the sexy atmosphere I saw in it. But it's all relaxed now."

"Yes, yes," de Gier said. "How much do you think this place is worth? Complete with all the trimmings I mean."

Grijpstra was still looking at the painting. "That painting is worth about ten guilders," he said, "it's a reproduction. But the frame is worth a few hundred. It's the only cheap item I have seen so far. A reproduction of a painting by Rousseau. Rousseau the customs officer. A chap like me. A government official earning a low salary. I wish I could paint."

"I didn't know you were interested in art," de Gier said. "You can still learn to paint. There are evening classes at the university."

"I know," Grijpstra said. "Maybe when I am pensioned off. I don't know anything about art but I know about this fellow. I read a book on his life and I have seen exhibitions of his work. He is a primitive painter. You want to know how much this place is worth?"

"Yes," de Gier said.

"A lot of money. These leather chairs are worth a few thousand guilders each. There are three of them, and there is a couch. Real leather. The carpet is worth money too. And this boat is about the best houseboat I have ever seen in Amsterdam. Good solid timber, two floors, must be over twenty meters long and over six wide. Two hundred thousand maybe, or more. It's a floating palace."

They had come to the kitchen. De Gier was again impressed. He thought of his own little kitchen, a large

cupboard with a mini-refrigerator and two hot plates. He
had learned to cook in it with his arms pressed to his chest.

"Nice kitchen, hey?" he asked Grijpstra, who was
looking at the gigantic fridge and the automatic stove with
its array of switches.

"Some people are really rich," Grijpstra said, "and
this is supposed to be a socialist country with the differ-
ences becoming smaller all the time. It would be interesting to find out what her source of income is."

"We will," de Gier said, "if anything has happened to
her. If not, we won't."

"Maybe she inherited the money," Grijpstra said in a
soothing voice.

They climbed the stairs. There was only one large room
upstairs, a very large room covering the full length and
width of the ship. The end of the staircase was a hole in the
floor of this room, fenced off on three sides by a railing
supported by carved wooden columns.

They were both careful not to touch anything, de Gier
had his hands in his pockets, Grijpstra's hands were folded
on his back.

Grijpstra sighed when he saw the woman on the floor.
She had collapsed on the thick white carpet. She had fallen
forward and they saw the long legs, the short skirt, the
white blouse and the flowing black hair spread partly on
the carpet, partly on the white blouse.

The blouse had a large red stain and the center of the
stain was the brass handle of a knife. Three large blue-
bottomed flies were buzzing through the room, their feeding disturbed by the arrival of the detectives.

2

THEY LOOKED at the dead woman and were impressed. De Gier was also a little sick. There was a smell, of course, a heavy smell which was turning his stomach. When he walked over to a window he staggered a little. He had to reach through the plants on the windowsill to find the handle of the window. It opened easily. He had remembered to use a handkerchief and to touch the handle at its end only. When he turned around the three fat flies were still buzzing about; there was an angry whine in their buzz. They had been feeding nicely and now there was movement in the room. They wanted to get back to the wound and the thick crusted blood.

"You phone," Grijpstra said hoarsely, and coughed. He had lowered his body into a low chair, close to the corpse. "I'll wait here."

De Gier rushed down the stairs, to the phone which he had seen in the large sitting room downstairs. He reported, put the phone down, and looked through the window. The small square-set figure of Bart de Jong was waiting at the end of the gangplank. He went outside.

"And?" Bart asked.

"I am afraid your neighbor is dead," de Gier said.

Bart said nothing. The beady black eyes showed no expression at all.

"Knife in her back," de Gier said.

Bart shook his head. "Violence," he said slowly, "that's wrong. We shouldn't hurt each other. Not even when we ask for it."

"Was she asking for it?" de Gier said.

Bart nodded.

"Why?"

"You don't know anything about her?" Bart asked.

"No. You tell me. You are her neighbor. Did you know her?"

"Oh sure. I knew her. The cat connected us. I used to bring the cat back and she would ask me in for a cup of coffee. A quick cup of coffee, we weren't friends, just neighbors."

"Didn't you make up to her?" de Gier asked surprised. "She seems to be an attractive woman."

Bart laughed. "No, I didn't try. I am not very good with women. I have no courage. They have to ask me, you know. Make their purpose plain, and even then I'll ask for permission to make quite sure it's all right."

De Gier smiled. He remembered that the man's hand had shaken when he lit a cigarette five minutes ago. Perhaps he was shy, didn't like to be confronted with others.

"You live by yourself?" he asked. Bart pointed at his houseboat. "The boat is quite small, as you can see. Only room for one person. I don't like to have visitors, the place gets too full, we fall over each other's legs."

"I see," de Gier said, "but why was she asking for violence?"

Bart didn't answer.

"Don't you want to tell me?"

"Not really," Bart said. "Why say unpleasant things about people?"

"She is dead," de Gier reminded him, "murdered. By somebody. We'll have to find him. If we don't he may kill somebody else. Society has to protect itself. You are part of the society. So am I."

Bart frowned.

"You don't agree?"

"No. Society is all balls. A lot of egotists thinking of themselves only. Insects locked in a bottle and all they can do is bite each other."

De Gier thought about the statement. He nodded slowly. "Perhaps you are right. But we can try not to bite each other."

"*She* bit others all right," Bart said.

"How?"

"Well, she was a whore you know. Slept with men who were prepared to give her money. A lot of money. Look at this boat."

"You don't approve of whores?" de Gier asked.

Some life came into Bart; he waved his right arm. "Yes, yes, I approve of them in a way. Men have to go somewhere to lose their energy. But they don't really enjoy going to whores. And the whores know it. They know how weak we are, we, the sperm-carriers."

"So they bite us," de Gier said.

"When they can. And this woman could. I have seen her clients leave her boat. They didn't look happy. She was sucking them dry. One of them must have been a violent man."

"And you are not a violent man?" de Gier asked.

"No. I wouldn't carry arms so I refused to join the army. I put up an act and they let me go after a few weeks. I cut my hands with a pocketknife and cried and wandered all over the barracks, bleeding."

"That's a violent act," de Gier said.

"Perhaps. It was a form of self-destruction, of course."

De Gier made an effort to control his temper. He had run into this sort of man before and they never failed to irritate him. He reminded himself that he shouldn't argue with the man.

"What do you do for a living?" he asked.

Bart shook his head.

"You are on unemployment benefits?" de Gier asked.

"For the last few months. I have had a lot of jobs but the boss always gets rid of me in the end. I was a van driver last."

De Gier saw the police cars nosing their way down the narrow road.

"My mates are coming. I would like you to go to your boat and wait for us, we may take a few hours."

"Am I under arrest?"

"Not really, just wait for us on your boat. You are the only person we have found so far who knew her. We'll have to ask some questions, we won't bother you longer than we have to."

Grijpstra had been sitting on the low chair, contemplating the dead woman. The silence of the room oppressed him. He badly wanted to get up and chase the large flies out of the window but he stuck to the chair, anxious not to destroy tracks. The room was bound to provide indications. He studied the handle of the knife, some six feet away from his eyes. He put on his glasses and concentrated on the patch of blood and its gleaming center. The copper of the handle shone as if it had been polished. "An army knife," he thought, "but why do I think that? We didn't have knives like that in the army." But he was still convinced it was an army knife and began to delve patiently in his memory. What other armies did he know? The German army. He concentrated and saw the German soldiers walking through the streets of Amsterdam, some thirty years ago now. They had no knives, only bayonets. The officers perhaps. He remembered the German naval officers, they had daggers. But the daggers had been different, they were decorated with tassels and the handles ended in a small knob with a carved swastika. Wrong army. What other armies did he know? The American army. The Canadian army. The English.

"Yes." He nodded to himself. He remembered the English commandos who had been in barracks close to the house where his parents lived. He had been allowed to accompany a few of them on a little trip through Holland and he had wanted to see their weapons. One of the soldiers had emptied the chamber of his revolver and given it to him and he had pulled the trigger a few times before returning it, and another soldier had given him his knife, a long cruel knife. The soldier had thrown it. They were having lunch under a few trees and the soldier had pointed at a tree and thrown the knife, which flashed in the sun and then stood in the tree's bark, trembling. Grijpstra had thrown the knife as well but he missed and the soldier laughed at him and cleaned the blade of the knife on his trouser leg and put it back carefully into its leather sheath. A wicked evil knife. A knife with a copper handle. A knife used for killing. Legal, authorized killing. The knife had been designed to kill enemies of the British people but now it had killed a Dutch citizen, born on the island of Curaçao, a small island in the Caribbean.

Had she been stabbed, Grijpstra wondered. Or had the knife been thrown? Had it trembled after it found its mark? He looked around him. It could have been thrown. Perhaps the lady hadn't known that she had a visitor. The killer could have crept up the steps, paused at the top of the staircase. The woman had her back to him. Swish! She would never have known who had killed her.

His eyes reported something unusual, a small red light. She had been sewing, using her machine. An electric machine, it had its warning light still on, must have been on for days on end. He shuddered. Another red eye was looking at him from across the room. It gleamed from the dial panel of a radio phonograph. The radio wasn't on so she must have been listening to a record. So she hadn't been able to hear her killer. A woman, peacefully engaged in her own room. Perhaps some crooner had been singing to her about his passion and about the moon and about flowers and then the winged dagger hit her.

He smiled. Winged dagger, very melodramatic. Good thing de Gier wasn't with him. Just the sort of thing de Gier would have said. De Gier was an incurable romantic. A heap of sand at the side of a street being ruined by Public Works would immediately remind him of the desert. And the desert would make him think of Arabs riding their camels on a raid. And before you knew where he was taking you, he would be raving about the eternal silence of space and the white rays of the moon and the quiet circling of majestic vultures. Winged dagger indeed. Still, the knife had flown through the air and it had hit this woman's back and cut the pulsing life inside her body.

A nice body, Grijpstra thought. But dead. He had seen a dead dog in the street the day before, run over by a city bus. He had known the dog well, a young playful Alsatian belonging to a window cleaner who lived a few houses down the street. He had often played with the dog but its dead body had been hard to connect with the living image that he remembered. Death is indeed the absolute end. A body becomes an object. And this woman's corpse was an object. But nicely shaped.

A prostitute, he thought. High class, but still a prostitute. She would have been very good at her profession. An American colonel, a Belgian diplomat, a Dutch tycoon. Her fees would have been high. How much would she have asked? A common whore asks twenty five guilders, and maybe a hundred if the customer has special requests. So how much would Mrs. van Buren have asked? Five hundred? A thousand?

Girjpstra grunted. A thousand! A laborer's wage. A

skilled man working for a full month would get that money. He took off his glasses and polished the lenses, looking balefully at the corpse.

But he corrected himself. He was merely surmising. Perhaps the poor woman hadn't charged at all. Perhaps she had invited men for company and they had used her and perhaps she had been grateful. In any case he, Grijpstra, shouldn't judge. He had to find the killer and produce a good round case so that the public prosecutor would know what to do. A simple task. No morals.

His mind at rest he began to look around him again. A pleasant room, lots of light, windows on three sides. A woman's room. She wouldn't receive her visitors up here. This was the room where she could be by herself and make dresses and listen to records and look after her plants. There were plants on all windowsills. He recognized some of them. Christ's-thorn, pig's ears, the shrimp plant with a pink growth at the end of each stalk. Some of the plants he didn't recognize. They looked like weeds. He searched his mind for knowledge about weeds. And as he was trying to think, the police cars arrived and began to maneuver for parking space outside.

The commissaris had arrived as well, and Grijpstra, who had left the boat to the photographers, the fingerprint men, and the doctor, was reporting with de Gier at his side, at a respectable distance but still part of this small inner circle.

"Dead hey?" the commissaris said. "So the Secret Service was right for once. The last time they used us we wasted three weeks on an old army uniform and that was all there was to find. Remember?"

"Yes sir," de Gier said. He had found the uniform. It had been discarded by an American sergeant in a hotel room. But the Secret Service had given the case top priority. There had been no case. There had been no secrets, no spies, nothing. But a lot of work, work in the dark, for neither Grijpstra nor de Gier nor the half dozen other policemen involved in the search had known what they were after. They had been given hazy orders and lots of addresses and they had tramped around until, one evening, they had been told that the alarm was false.

"Yes, I remember, sir," de Gier said again.

"But now they have guided us to a corpse," the commissaris said, "so maybe they have intelligence."

"A murdered corpse," Grijpstra said.

The commissaris smiled his old man's smile. The corners of his mouth moved.

"Well," he said, "I won't go in. They'll be busy for a while in there. I'll take your car and drive myself back and you can come home with the others. The chief inspector will be sorry to miss all this but I won't call him back. You and I will have to solve the case and he can sit in the sun for a few more weeks. Good day."

"Sir," the two men said, and de Gier gave the commissaris the keys of the gray VW.

The ambulance had arrived and the two brothers of the Health Service came out of the boat, carefully carrying their stretcher, followed by the police doctor.

"Morning," he said to Grijpstra. "She has been dead for two days at least. The knife went right in."

"Could it have been thrown in?" Grijpstra asked.

"Could be," the doctor said. "It's an unusual knife. Never seen one like it. I'll be able to tell you tomorrow."

"Has the body been moved, you think?" Grijpstra asked.

"No."

The doctor was close to his car when Grijpstra remembered the plants. He ran to the car.

"Excuse me, doctor. Do you know anything about plants?" The doctor looked startled. "Plants?"

"Yes. Plants. Weeds."

"I know a little," the doctor said. "You don't think she was poisoned, do you?"

Grijpstra explained what he meant.

"I see," the doctor said. "We'll have to go back."

Together they studied the potted plants with de Gier, mystified, in the background.

"Hmm," the doctor said.

Grijpstra waited.

"I am not sure," the doctor said. "I'll have to take them with me. They are weeds all right, and pretty nasty weeds, I should say. Poisonous."

Grijpstra grunted.

"How did you manage to notice them?" the doctor asked, turning around at the grunt. "You know anything about plants?"

"Not really," Grijpstra said, "but I had to spend some time in this room by myself and I thought these weeds looked like weeds, not like the sort of plant everybody has around."

"What's all this?" asked de Gier. "What are we? Botanists?"

"Have you never heard about weeds, friend?" the doctor asked, looking at de Gier pleasantly.

"I have heard about *the* weed," de Gier said, "and I have some geraniums on my balcony, and something with little white flowers which my aunt gave me. Asylum I think it is called."

"Alyssum," the doctor said. "Fifty cents a plant on the street market. Bought some myself the other day, very pretty, heavy smell of honey. But these weeds are different. If they are what I think they are they are poisonous. There are three types, you see. I'll check them out with a friend of mine; he also works for the city, assistant chief of all our parks. He should know."

"Poisonous, you say," Grijpstra said.

The doctor lit his pipe and looked at the plants again. "Poisonous, for sure. But perhaps they can be used for other purposes. A witch might make a love potion out of them. Or an ointment. If you rub the ointment in your armpits and all over your penis and balls you may have some interesting sensations."

"Yes?" de Gier asked.

"You might find yourself flying through the sky, my friend, on a broomstick, on your way to a party."

Grijpstra put a heavy hand on de Gier's shoulder. "Wouldn't you like that, de Gier?" he asked.

"I would," de Gier said.

"There would be plenty of fun at the party," the doctor said.

"What sort of fun?" de Gier asked, staring at the plants with bulging eyes.

"Sex," the doctor said. "Good clean sex."

"Boy!" de Gier said.

"You can help me carry them down to my car."

A little later de Gier was staggering down the stairs holding the largest pot. The doctor had a smaller pot, and Grijpstra was carrying a very small pot, gingerly, as if the innocent-looking weed would explode in his face.

"A witch," de Gier was mumbling to himself.

3

"WHAT I LIKE about the police," de Gier said, "is our teamwork."

Grijpstra looked at the last car leaving the small parking area near the houseboat. He looked thoughtful.

"You shouldn't have lent our car to the commissaris," he said.

"Ha," de Gier said.

Together they walked to the small houseboat which housed their first suspect, Bart de Jong. They walked slowly.

"You have any ideas yet?" de Gier asked.

Grijpstra produced a large dirty white handkerchief and sneezed in it.

"Don't sneeze. Answer me."

Grijpstra sneezed again. De Gier jumped back. It was a loud sneeze and expressed Grijpstra's contempt of the world.

"Ideas," Grijpstra said. "Yes. Why not? The lady is a prostitute, we are told. Suppose she is a prostitute, she probably is, so we can safely suppose. Prostitutes don't like their customers, in fact they hate them. They blame their clients for what they are, and they are right. Everybody is always right, we mustn't forget that. It's a basic truth. So the prostitute hates her client and makes him feel her power. He needs her. He comes back. He doesn't really want to come back but he does, because he has to. His desire is much stronger than his will power. She sees him coming back and she humiliates him. The client doesn't want to be humiliated. The client is right too. He tries to hurt her. And killing is an extreme form of hurting."

They were walking through a piece of virgin land and de Gier stopped. He looked at the weeds growing around his feet. "Do you think these weeds are dangerous?" he asked.

Grijpstra looked at the weeds de Gier was pointing at. "No. I used to work for a farmer when I was a boy, during the summer holidays. I had to clear land for him. I remember some of the weeds. That's pig's grass, I recognize the black spots on the leaves. You see?"

De Gier saw the black spots. "What did she need those weeds for?" he asked.

Grijpstra turned to his friend and looked mean. Grijpstra was good at looking mean for he often had to read stories to his two youngest children and they liked him to pull faces as he read. He now pulled his meanest face, reserved for really wicked characters. He bared his big square teeth, lowered his eyelids and twisted his upper lip so that the ends of his bristly mustache came up a little.

"She wanted to put a spell on her clients," he hissed.

"Sha," de Gier said, "don't do that."

"Do what?"

"Talk like that."

"I wasn't talking like that," Grijpstra said. "I was trying to explain something."

"Do you think she can fly on a broomstick?" de Gier asked.

"Could," Grijpstra said. "She is dead now."

"Her soul is still alive," de Gier said, and shuddered.

Grijpstra didn't reply. He had seen the shudder and was wondering whether the shudder was real. He had never been able to really get to know his colleague, for as soon as Grijpstra had labeled de Gier's behavior and fitted him into a certain pattern, de Gier would do something in direct opposition to the newly found definition. But perhaps, Grijpstra thought, the shudder was real. They had, after all, discovered Mrs. van Buren's dead body that morning and there had been the smell and the three evil blue-bottomed, gigantic flies. And de Gier had been nauseated. Since then they had discovered the weeds, witch weeds, black-magic weeds.

They had reached the door of the small houseboat. The door opened as de Gier reached for the bell.

"Sorry it took so long," de Gier said.

Bart smiled. "It's all right, please come in. You can have some coffee if you like."

"That would be very nice," Grijpstra said gratefully.

"You can have some sandwiches as well," Bart said.

"That would be even nicer."

The houseboat consisted of one room only. Bart cut the bread and poured coffee.

The boat's interior was remarkable, remarkable because there was hardly anything in the boat. The walls, made of large strong planks, were painted white and left bare. There was a large table and a chair and a wooden bench on which the policemen were now sitting, looking neat and obedient, like boys at a well-disciplined school. There were some books on the table. De Gier got up and looked at them. Three had been written by highbrow writers and the other two contained reproductions of modern paintings. All five books had been borrowed from the public library. There was a bed in the boat, an army bed, and the mattress and blankets were army as well. A corner of the room was arranged as the kitchen. There was an old fridge, a simple electric stove and a large sink, and another table on which Bart was now preparing a salad. There was also an easel with a half-finished painting.

"You like olives?" Bart asked.

"No, thanks," Grijpstra said.

"Please," de Gier said.

"I like to cook," Bart explained as he quickly set the table. "If I had known you would be coming for lunch I would have produced something better. I have two good meals every day, it makes up for being alone."

"You have never been married?" Grijpstra asked.

"Yes. A long time ago now."

"Any children?" Grijpstra asked.

"No. I wouldn't have left her if there had been any children, I think. My father left me when I was a baby."

"I see," Grijpstra said.

"Nice boat," de Gier said, taking a bite out of the thick slice of freshly baked bread which Bart had amply covered with a piece of smoked sausage and a lettuce leaf, "but a bit bare."

"A poor man can't afford to have things," Bart said.

De Gier shook his head. "I don't agree," he said, "I have been poor but I have always had things. Too many, in fact. Clutter the place up. God knows where they come from but before you know it the room is full of them and you have to start throwing them away. And *you* live in an empty boat. How do you manage living without things?"

"Oh, I don't know," Bart said. "I *do* have things. Bed, table, chair, a complete kitchen. I paint and I need brushes and canvas and frames and lots of paints, of course. I have all that. And there's a cupboard over there which you haven't seen yet, there's a gramophone in it and an electric heater and clothes and a few odds and ends."

De Gier was still shaking his head. "You have the

absolutely necessary," he said, "but where's the rest?"

Bart laughed. "You really want me to explain my way of life? Are you interested in people?"

"I am," de Gier said.

"Of course he is," Grijpstra added, "he is very interested in people. So am I."

"You are policemen," Bart said, "representatives of the State. Have you ever realized that we, ordinary citizens, think of you as representatives of the State? That we think, every time we see a cop, 'there's the State'?"

"We do," Grijpstra said.

"Yes," Bart said, "perhaps you do. You are probably intelligent. It's a pity. A civilian may think 'there's the State' but he will also think 'ah well, cops are stupid.' But maybe he is wrong. Perhaps cops are not so stupid."

"Please explain your way of life," de Gier said.

Bart poured more coffee from his tin jug. "I am a misfit, that's my explanation. But I know I am. I'll never be able to hold a job. I start working, I try to fit in, I do my best but after a while it goes wrong and I get fired. When I do work I earn the minimal wage and when I lose the job I only get a percentage, so whatever I do, I'll never have any money."

"So?" de Gier asked.

"So I don't spend any. It's possible to live quite comfortably on little money. It's a discovery I made a long time ago. It needs discipline, that's all. I say 'no' all the time. I buy food, of course. Good food. And tobacco. Food and tobacco have their price and I have to pay it. But all the other stuff I don't buy."

"You bought the furniture," Grijpstra said, "and the kitchen utensils, and the blankets and whatever you have in your cupboard."

"I did. But I paid very little. It came from auctions and dump stores. I save half of what I get, wages and unemployment money. I have an old bicycle for transport. This boat I built myself, years ago. The boat itself I stole from the ship's cemetery on the river. I think the man in charge saw me take her but he didn't mind. There are a lot of boats over there and they are rotting away. I had to rebuild the superstructure and I had to buy some materials but not much. I don't think I spent more than half a year's savings and since then it has saved me a good sum in rent.''

De Gier had got up and was looking out of the window. A large barge came past, being pulled by an energetic little river tug.

De Gier was thinking of his own flat in the suburbs. He was also thinking of all the money he had wasted over the years. The day before, in fact: two striped shirts he didn't need, and at a very fancy price.

"What the hell," he thought and turned around. "But you paint," he said.

"Yes. I do, and I have never been able to figure out a way of buying paint cheaply. I try not to waste paint.''

Grijpstra had walked over to the easel. "Can I look at your work?"

"Sure.''

The painting showed a building. Grijpstra recognized the building, it had never occurred to him that there was anything special about it, a large lumpy heap of bricks and plaster, built during the depression of 1929 by the city for one of its many departments. The painting was very realistic, minute in detail. But Grijpstra found that he liked the painting and he kept looking at it.

"Do you paint yourself?" Bart asked.

"No. But I would like to.''

"Why don't you then?''

"Ah!" Grijpstra made a gesture. "Why don't I paint? I work, I come home, I read the paper, I go to sleep. There are lots of things I would like to do, but the children take time and my wife talks to me and the TV is on. I go fishing sometimes, but that's all.''

"Pity," Bart said.

"Yes, pity. I like your painting but I don't know why.''

"Look again," Bart said.

"The contrast maybe," Grijpstra said. "The grays and the whites. It makes the building look like it ought to have looked."

"No," Bart said. "It does look that way. Late in the day, just before the light goes. It has a life of its own and I am trying to catch it. It also has a row of ventilators on its roof which turn around all the time. I haven't done the ventilators yet, it'll be very difficult to get their movement. The best thing would be to cut small holes into the canvas and make little metal ventilators and build them in, and make them turn around. I could install a little electric motor."

"No, no," Grijpstra said, "it would become a pop thing. You'll cheapen it."

"Perhaps."

De Gier was now also looking at the painting. "It might be very good," de Gier said, "but it's not original. I have seen paintings of windmills and the mill's sails turned."

"Nothing is original," Bart said. "Whatever you do has been done before. Only our combinations are our own but even combinations have been done before. I am sure someone else, at this very moment, is thinking of building rotating metal miniature ventilators into a two-dimensional painting."

"Yes," Grijpstra said.

"You really want to know about Mrs. van Buren's death, don't you?" Bart asked.

"And about her life," de Gier said.

Bart was rolling himself a cigarette from a dented tin. His hands weren't shaking.

"I can't tell you about her death. Do you know when she died?"

"Not the exact time," de Gier said, "but the doctor will be able to tell us tomorrow."

"Well, whatever the exact time was, I am sure I won't have an alibi. I am always by myself and it would be easy for me to sneak over to her boat and kill her. Easier for me than for anybody else for I can see her boat from my windows and I could find out whether she was alone or not. How did she die?"

"I told you already," de Gier said. "Somebody put a knife in her back."

"Ah yes, a knife. I would never use a knife."

"What would you use?"

"Nothing, I wouldn't kill. I would let them kill me. Perhaps I would kill to protect my child but I don't have a child. I wouldn't protect myself."

"So you don't know anything about her death," de Gier said. "Well, tell us about her life."

Bart shook his head. "I told you already. I never got to know her very well. She has had me in there for coffee but there was never any conversation. I have some geraniums and they weren't doing well and she told me to put some special plant stuff in the water, she even gave me a carton full of it. I often fed her cat so perhaps she wanted to do something in return."

"Will you be looking after the cat now?" de Gier asked.

"Are you concerned?"

"Yes," de Gier said. "I have a cat myself."

"Don't worry. I'll look after the cat. It'll mess the boat up with all its hair but I'll keep him if nobody else wants him."

"Good," de Gier said.

"Who do you think killed her?" Grijpstra asked.

"One of her clients maybe?"

"Perhaps. Do you know who they are?"

Bart thought for nearly half a minute. "No. I can describe their cars. A new black Citroën with a CD plate and a Belgian number. A big Buick with a USA number, must be some army officer stationed in Germany; and another Citroën, also new, with real leather upholstery and a lot of chromium plating, a silver-colored car. I don't have the numbers. There were always the same cars. I often wondered what would happen if they arrived at the same time but they never did. She must have received them by strict appointment.''

"Did anyone else ever visit her?''

Bart thought again. "Yes. The man with the red waist-coat. He used to come on Sunday mornings. A fat chap with a face like one of those small Edam cheeses, no expression at all on it. And he always wore a dark red velvet waistcoat with a gold watch-chain. I couldn't make out what he came for. He used to have a small boy with him, five years old maybe, and he always came on Sunday mornings. Sometimes he came without the boy.''

"Did he come by car?''

"No. On foot, with the boy.''

"And when he was without the boy?''

"Also on foot.''

"Tall man? Small man?''

"Just under six foot and getting fat. Forty years old, going bald. I could make a sketch.''

Bart made a sketch, quickly, in pencil. The drawing was well done.

"Draw in the little boy as well, please,'' Grijpstra said.

"Why? The little boy wouldn't put a knife into a woman!''

"No, but we'll show the drawing around. Perhaps somebody will recognize them.''

Bart drew in the little boy.

"He is carrying a ball under his arm,'' de Gier said.

"That's right. The boy always had a ball.''

"Anyone else?'' de Gier asked.

"No one else I can think of. She did have other visitors but I can't remember them. Not clients anyway. Trades-men perhaps and delivery boys and Jehovah's Witnesses, they always come around, they seem to like us, and a man selling eggs and door-to-door salesmen and people who have lost their way.''

"And yourself," de Gier said.

"That's right." Bart looked relaxed.

"We won't bother you any longer," Grijpstra said. "Thanks for the lunch. Where's the nearest tram stop please?"

"You don't have a car?" Bart asked, surprised.

"The commissaris took it."

Bart laughed. "Walk down the path and turn left at the end, you'll have to walk to the football stadium and catch a tram from there. There's a taxi stand over there as well."

"You're joking," de Gier said.

"You never asked him if he had seen her flying on a broomstick," Grijpstra said as they walked down the long path to the main road.

4

"DO COME IN," the commissaris said pleasantly. The four men trooped in, smiling. They shook hands. They accepted cigars. They lit one anothers' cigars. But they were tense.

"I am glad you could come immediately," the commissaris said and sat down while he waved a small hand in the direction of chairs. The commissaris had a good room at Headquarters. He shared his rank with four other officers but he was the oldest and ranked directly under the chief constable and he had used his stars to secure comfortable quarters, with a thick rug on the floor, old paintings on the walls, a lot of large potted plants, and his own private coffee machine.

"We contacted the colonel by Telex yesterday afternoon," the man from the American embassy said.

The man directly opposite the commissaris bristled a little, reminding the commissaris of a large bear. A grizzly bear he thought it was, he had seen a stuffed specimen once in the zoological museum. The colonel looked friendly but dangerous. His thick tweed suit, not very suitable for the hot day they were having, accentuated the impression.

"You didn't contact *me*," he said to the man of the embassy, speaking rather loudly, too loudly the commissaris thought, "you made contact with the military police and they took me here."

The two other men said nothing.

"True or not?" the colonel asked the two silent men.

"Not quite, sir," the younger of the two said. "We invited you to come."

"And if I had refused?"

"You didn't refuse, sir," the military policeman said.

The commissaris smiled. He was enjoying himself. Policemen all over the world have common traits. He would have said the same thing under the circumstances.

"We won't keep you longer than necessary," the commissaris said softly. "Let me tell you why we invited you to come here."

The colonel relaxed a little. The commissaris had made a good impression.

"I know why I am here," the colonel said. "I was told by your colleagues. Maria van Buren is dead. Somebody murdered her. She was a friend of mine."

"Quite," the commissaris said. "She was your girl friend. We found her with a knife in her back. A dagger, in fact. A military knife. She was killed between eight P.M. and twelve P.M. last Saturday according to our police doctor."

The colonel thought. He thought for a full minute and broke out in a wide smile. "Last Saturday I was in Düsseldorf, I spent the night there, with friends. I don't think I spent a minute by myself that day and I wasn't alone during the night either. And I can prove what I am telling you."

"Good," the commissaris said, "I am very pleased on your behalf."

But the colonel wasn't listening. He was looking out of

the window, the wide smile still on his face. When he had
finished looking out of the window he turned and faced the
two military police officers.

"Ha," he said, "you are wasting your time on me. If
you had waited I could have proved my alibi in Germany."

The commissaris didn't give his colleagues a chance to
answer back. "Now, now," he said smoothly, "we didn't
invite you to come here to prove that you have committed a
murder. At this stage of the investigation we merely want
information. We know almost nothing about the dead
woman. You knew her well. Perhaps you wouldn't mind
telling us about her."

"Please, colonel," the man from the embassy said. The
commissaris glanced at the man from the embassy. A nice
young man, he thought. Very helpful.

"O.K., O.K.," the colonel said, "please excuse me. I
didn't want to be difficult but I have been under some
strain ever since these two gentlemen came to see me and
never left me for a minute. I think they even kept me under
observation when I went to the toilet in the plane. Thought
that I might squeeze through the window."

The military policemen laughed politely and stopped
laughing at the same moment.

"O.K. I'll help. I knew Maria well, intimately as they
say. For three years now. Used to come to Amsterdam at
least once a month. I am stationed just across the border, it
isn't a very long drive. I am sorry she is dead."

"Please excuse me," the commissaris said, "but you
don't look sorry."

The colonel scratched his knee. "I don't?"

"No. You look relieved."

"Well, I am relieved that I can prove that I didn't kill
her."

"I see," the commissaris said.

"All right," the colonel said, "maybe I am relieved. I
don't have to go and see her anymore."

"Were you tiring of her?"

"You speak very good English, you know," the colonel said.

The commissaris smiled. "Most Dutchmen do. We have to; this is a small country in a big world and nobody speaks Dutch, except us."

"Would you like to pour us all another cup of coffee?" the commissaris asked the young man from the embassy. The young man jumped from his chair, eager to oblige.

"Were you tiring of her?"

"Tiring," the colonel said, "no. But I did want to get away from her."

"But that would be easy," the commissaris said, "all you had to do was stop seeing her."

The colonel was scratching his knee again.

"Are you married?" the commissaris asked.

"Yes. In the States. My wife used to be with me in Germany but she went home again. She knew about Maria, if that's what you mean. Maria wasn't blackmailing me, she couldn't because I told my wife about her."

"Would she have blackmailed you if you hadn't told your wife?"

The colonel began to scratch his other knee. "She might have."

"Would you say that Maria van Buren wasn't a very nice woman?" the commissaris asked.

The colonel nodded. "Yes," he said slowly, "I could say that. But she was very attractive. Beautiful too, but a lot of women are beautiful without being attractive. Beauty becomes boring sometimes."

"Are you an expert?" the commissaris asked.

The colonel laughed. "I am supposed to be an expert in the army. I should know something about atomic warheads. Maybe I also know something about women."

"So Mrs. van Buren attracted you and you went to see her regularly but now you are pleased that you don't have to see her again. Perhaps you could explain your relationship a little.''

The colonel shifted in his chair. He had stopped scratching his knees and his hands were looking for some other activity. He became aware of his hands and put them in the pockets of his jacket.

''Were you paying the lady, sir?'' the youngest military policeman asked.

''Yes, I was paying her.''

''A lot?'' the commissaris asked.

''She wasn't cheap.''

''How much were you paying her?''

''All right,'' the colonel said, ''she was a whore, if you must know. A high-class whore. She charged five hundred a night, payable in advance. Cash on the barrelhead or no fun and games. But her fun and games were good.''

''Dollars?''

''No, guilders. But five hundred guilders is a lot of money. And there were extras. Perfume, a ring, a dress. A fur coat too. The fur coat was two thousand dollars, but I wanted her very badly then.''

The face of the older military policeman moved. It moved for a few seconds and suddenly a question popped out of the face.

''Did she ever show any interest in your job, sir?''

''No,'' the colonel snapped, ''she never asked me about atomic warheads.''

''These questions must be very unpleasant for you,'' the commissaris said, ''and we won't ask many more, but I have been calculating a little. If you knew the lady for three years, and if she charged five hundred guilders per visit, and if you saw her at least once a month, and if you gave her expensive presents, you must have spent some ten thousand dollars on her.''

''That's correct,'' the colonel said. ''I worked it out myself on the plane. Ten thousand.''

"That's real money," the commissaris said. "Would you mind telling us how and where you met her?"

"I met her at a party. I often used to come to Amsterdam before I met Maria. Amsterdam is a good town for us, better than Germany. The atmosphere is just right here. I used to come with friends of mine and one of them knew some people here. There's an old gable house on the Leidse Gracht which belongs to a rich Dutchman, a man called Drachtsma. His first name is Ice, I think, something like that. The name suits him, he is a very cool guy. There were a lot of people at the party, some of them pretty famous, I believe. Musicians, painters, big businessmen, professors. They like to have foreigners at the house. Maria was the star of the party and I was careful because she seemed to be Ice's girlfriend but she made it real easy for me. I took her to her houseboat that night and stayed."

"Did she make you pay?"

"She did," the colonel said. "It made me feel silly all right. I thought I was making a big impression but I had to pay."

"And you kept going back," the commissaris said, "even when you didn't really want to anymore. That's right, isn't it?"

"That's right," the colonel said.

"Illogical, isn't it?"

"Yes. I can't explain it. It wasn't love. It was sex, of course, but I can get sex in Germany."

"Do you know of any other men who were interested in Mrs. van Buren?" the commissaris asked.

"Anybody who knows her, I would guess," the colonel said. "You would have been if you had known her."

The commissaris smiled. "I am an old man," he said, "and I suffer from rheumatism."

"She would have cured it perhaps."

"Yes. She might have. But she is dead."

"Well, Ice was interested in her, the man who gave the

party and who owned the house. Big man with a bald head. A big powerful man. I am sure she was his mistress as well."

"Wasn't that difficult? Sharing her with others, I mean?"

"Not really. I could only see her if she wanted to see me."

"Did you ever visit her without an appointment?"

"I tried once, she didn't open her door, but the lights were on. There was a car parked on the other side of the path. A black Citroën with a CD plate."

"Did you know the owner of the car?"

"No."

"Weren't you jealous?"

"No," the colonel said. "No, I don't think I was. I felt silly that was all."

"You have used the word 'silly' before. She often made you feel silly, didn't she?"

The colonel didn't reply.

The commissaris put on his kind old man's face.

"Don't feel embarrassed," he said. "We are all men in this room. We know what it is to feel silly."

"O.K.," the colonel said, "she made me feel silly a lot."

The commissaris got up. "Thank you for coming," he said. "Here is my card. If anything else occurs to you, anything which may help us to find our man, let us know."

They shook hands. The colonel and the young man from the embassy left.

"Interesting," the commissaris said to the two military police officers.

"Very," the older replied. "You'll find your man all right. A nice straightforward case, I would say. A client has killed her, don't you think? Or a client's right hand. It must be possible to hire a killer, even in Amsterdam."

"Why *even* in Amsterdam?" the commissaris asked.

"Nice easy town. Quiet. I hear you don't even have a proper homicide squad here. You only have one when there is a murder and you only have a few murders a year. I am from the States, it's different where I come from."

"Yes," the commissaris said, "perhaps this will be an easy case. But we found no fingerprints, and the weapon is a professional weapon. A British commando knife. The doctor thinks it was thrown and there aren't many citizens in Amsterdam who can throw a commando knife."

"I would rather have your case than ours," the youngest officer said.

"You have a case?"

"You know what the colonel is doing, he told you."

"Atomic warheads," the commissaris said. "Our Secret Service is interested. They led us to the case. We were watching the houseboat long before the woman was killed."

"Exactly," the officer said. "The colonel has some secrets, and the woman had him in the hollow of her little hand."

"So what will you do now?" the commissaris said.

The two policemen got up and began to walk to the door.

"Watch him," the older officer said. "If he spends ten thousand dollars on a whore he isn't a very good security risk."

"Who is?" the commissaris asked.

"He didn't do it," Grijpstra said.

"No," de Gier said.

They had a long drive, three hours to the north and nearly three hours to the south, they were almost back in Amsterdam.

"Nice chap," Grijpstra was saying, "a happy man. Happy in his job, happily married."

"Sickening, isn't it?" de Gier asked.

"No. Why? Men should be happy."

"It isn't natural."

"Perhaps not," Grijpstra agreed, "but it is nice to see an exception, to actually meet one in the flesh. I really liked the man."

"But it was a wasted trip," de Gier said moodily, trying to overtake a large truck which was wavering slightly.

"He is asleep. Honk your horn."

De Gier honked. A hand appeared from the cabin's window and waved them on.

"Saved his life," Grijpstra said. "Must have been driving for more than his legal eight hours. You could stop him and ask him to produce his logbook."

"No," de Gier said, "this is an unmarked car, you have been in uniform too long."

"Right," Grijpstra said. "Let's sum up. We went to see Maria van Buren's former husband. He married her in Curaçao, ten years ago, when she was twenty-four. They spent a year on the island together and came to Holland. He took her to the North where he got a job as a director of a textile factory. She was bored. She liked him, and she liked pottering about in the garden, and she did a bit of sailing on the lakes and she visited the islands, but she was bored all the same. He didn't have much time to spend on her so she took to sailing by herself. She was often gone for the day. She started staying away for the nights as well. She spent an occasional weekend in Amsterdam by herself. He objected and they were divorced. No children. He married again, six years ago and he is happy. His new wife is nice, we met her. We saw the children, a toddler and a baby. Nice children. He used to pay alimony but she wrote to him and told him he didn't have to send her money so he stopped. That was three years ago. He hasn't seen her since they were divorced. And most important of all, he has an alibi. He couldn't have been in Amsterdam on Saturday, or on Friday, or on Sunday. He wasn't there so he didn't kill her. He didn't have any reason to kill her either. And he seemed genuinely sorry that she had been murdered. I believed him. Didn't you?"

"Sure," de Gier said. "I believed him, and I never believe an ex-husband when his former wife has been murdered. Husbands and ex-husbands are always prime suspects in a murder case."

"Yes," Grijpstra said heavily. "So what else did this prime suspect tell us?"

"That she comes from a good family. Curaçao high society. Her father is an important businessman. He is still alive, so is her mother. She has several sisters, all beauties. They sent her to Holland and she went to high school here and spent a few years at a university, studying Dutch literature. We'll have to ask the Curaçao police to find out what they can. That'll be easy, we can get them on the Telex and we can phone. I have telephoned to Curaçao before, there's only a few minutes' delay."

"So what else?"

"Nothing else," de Gier said. "We have wasted a day."

"It's impossible to waste a day," Grijpstra said. "We did something, didn't we?"

"We could have stayed home," de Gier said. "It's nice to stay at home. I could have read a book on the balcony of my flat. It has been a beautiful sunny day. I could have talked to my cat and I could have gone to a nursery. I want some more plants on my balcony."

"Plants," Grijpstra said. "I spoke to the doctor before we left. He checked those weeds with his friend. You know what they were?"

"No. You know I don't know what they were."

"One was belladonna, one was deadly nightshade, and the third was datura or thorn apple."

"So?"

"Poisonous. All three of them. And they are used by sorcerers."

"Botanists," de Gier said. "I told you we would become botanists."

"Not botanists," Grijpstra said. "We'll have to become sorcerers."

5

THAT SAME EVENING, close to midnight, a large black sedate car was heading for Amsterdam, forty-five minutes away from The Hague, where it had spent an hour parked in front of the Belgian embassy.

The commissaris was asleep on the back seat, his frail body slumped against Grijpstra. Grijpstra was awake and moodily contemplating the dark fields flashing past and remembering the evening's long fruitless conversation, and de Gier and the constable driver were whispering to each other on the front seat.

"I can't keep my eyes open," the young constable whispered to de Gier. "It's hopeless, I am no good as a driver. I have put in my fourth application for a transfer but it will be refused again for the commissaris seems to like me. I have almost killed him and myself and people in other cars, I have driven the car off the road half a dozen times, I have fallen asleep waiting for traffic lights to change color but he won't give in. He says I'll get used to it. I'll never get used to it. The sound of an engine makes me sleepy, I get sleepy as soon as I turn the starter key. And I am sleepy now.''

"Shall I hit you in the face?" de Gier asked.

"Won't help. I only stay awake when somebody talks to me. Tell me a story, sergeant.''

"A story?" de Gier asked. "What sort of story?"

"Anything," the constable said, "but try and make it a good story. You investigate crimes, don't you? You should know lots of good stories. Or you can talk football to me. I am serious, you know. I am falling asleep; I have been on duty since seven o'clock this morning.''

"Some driver," de Gier said.

"I told you I shouldn't be a driver. Now will you tell me a story or do you prefer me to smash up the car? We are doing exactly a hundred kilometers an hour and it is a heavy car. She'll probably bounce off the steel rail on our left and turn over a few times. The passenger on the front seat always gets hurt worst.''

"Why didn't you sleep in the car while you were waiting for us at the embassy?"

"I tried, but I can't sleep when the car is stationary. It's the combination of movement and the sound of the engine that gets me. Look at my eyelids, they are half down. I can't control the muscles.''

De Gier sighed. "Once upon a time, some ten years ago, two years after I had become a uniformed constable doing street duty, we had a murderer in the inner city.''

"That's it," the constable said, "go on. I am listening.''

"We never saw him but we found his tracks and there were witnesses and gradually we built up a picture of what the murderer was supposed to look like, but it was difficult for he only killed late at night, in dark narrow alleys where nobody lives. The alleys are only alive during the day when the merchants move their stocks in and out of their warehouses; at night nobody goes there except cheap prostitutes and their clients. The few people who claimed to have caught a glimpse of the killer gave strange descriptions. This murderer didn't have teeth like you or me but fangs. He didn't walk, he bounced, with great leaping strides, and he had long black hair and a thick curly beard and bloodshot small eyes, and he dressed in a long black duffelcoat with a hood. Are you listening?''

"Sure, sure," the constable at the wheel said. "Go on, sergeant.''

"He only killed women and we used to find the corpses in the morning. He had torn them apart and their limbs were scattered all over the alleys. We found out that he would climb the gables of the warehouses and flatten himself on a windowsill so that he would be no more than a black blob and when the women walked underneath him he would jump them. Sometimes he would throttle them and sometimes he would bite right through their necks, tearing the veins and the muscles.''

"Jesus," the constable muttered.

"Yes," de Gier said, speaking in a very low whisper, almost hissing the words, "in those days we had real crimes. But it got too bad, one night the murderer killed two women and the commissaris decided to go all out and catch him.''

"You said you found his tracks," the constable whispered. "What did you find? Footprints? Fingerprints?''

"He wore gloves," de Gier said, "but we did find his footprints where he had walked through the blood of his victims. We decided that he was a very big man, well over six feet tall and powerfully built. And we always found peanut shells.''

"Peanut shells?''

"Yes. We also found the empty paper bags. It seemed he lived on peanuts for we would find as many as six bags in one spot where he would have been waiting for some time. The bags were traced to the Chinese quarter, where there were a lot of unemployed people at that time. The Chinese bought cheap peanuts in bulk and roasted them and then sold them on the street for next to nothing."

"So the commissaris decided to catch him, hey?" the constable said. "Which commissaris? Our commissaris?"

"The very man," de Gier said, turning around to look at the back seat where the commissaris was snoring gently, supported by Grijpstra's arm.

"What did he do?" the constable asked.

"He mobilized the entire police force. We had some six hundred men in the old city that night. Everybody had to come, even useless types like clerks and subinspectors and drivers. We had been properly armed for the occasion and all the constables had carbines. The sergeants and adjutants carried submachine guns and hand grenades and I was in charge of three men who knew how to fight with a flame thrower. The mounted men came with us and their horses were snorting all around. Behind us we could hear the motor cops, they still had Harley Davidsons in those days, and the engines, in first gear, growled. The armored cars of the military police had come out as well and their metal tracks grinding over the cobblestones caused sparks which lit up the alleys; the half-tracks looked very spectacular and the moonlight made the helmets of the drivers glint. We had a general warrant and had been given keys to all the warehouses and the detectives who were following us searched every building, every house. The boats of the State Water Police had joined us too, they were blocking the canals in case the killer should try to escape us in the water. We could hear their diesel engines idling as we were sneaking through the narrow streets on our thick rubber soles."

"So?" the constable whispered.

"It was the biggest operation I have been part of," de Gier said, "and it went on all night but we never had a glance of him. He must have stayed in his lair, sharpening his fangs with a file and doing physical exercises to keep fit."

"Some story," the constable said in a loud voice.

"Shhh, you'll wake up the commissaris," de Gier whispered. "I haven't finished yet. The commissaris was frustrated of course, but he didn't give in. He never does. He locked himself into his room for two days and thought and nobody was allowed to disturb him, not even his pet driver whom he was very fond of. And after two days he came out with a plan."

"A plan," the constable repeated.

"A psychological plan. He called Grijpstra and myself and three other men and told Grijpstra that he would have to go into the inner city by himself that night. Grijpstra did. We followed him, of course, but at a distance. Grijpstra had been given a large paper bag of the very best freshly roasted peanuts and we were all carrying bags as well, to give to Grijpstra in case he shouldn't have enough. The commissaris had told him that he should be eating peanuts all the time and talk to himself. He had to say, 'marvelous peanuts these' and 'very fresh, these peanuts, nice and crackly' and 'boy! I have never eaten such delicious peanuts in all my life.' "

"Peanuts," the constable repeated in a suspicious voice.

"Peanuts. Grijpstra had eaten four bags of peanuts and just started on his fifth when the killer rushed him. All we saw was a dark shadow flashing past. He tried to hit Grijpstra in the neck and to grab the bag at the same time but Grijpstra was alert and sidestepped and tripped him up. We were all on him at the same time and we threw a net over him, a special net which the commissaris had ordered from a firm which makes nets for catching sharks. It was a terrible fight and he nearly got away but we did manage to subdue him. Even Grijpstra helped although he was suffering from shock and full of peanuts and finally we overpowered the killer."

"Who was he?" the constable asked.

"I'll tell you some other time," de Gier said, changing

his voice to normal. "You can drop me off here, I live in this street. You actually managed to reach Amsterdam. Congratulations."

The car stopped and the commissaris woke up. "Are you getting out, de Gier?" he asked.

"Yes, sir. I live here."

"Why don't you come home with me, you and Grijp-stra. I live close by and you can walk home afterwards and Grijpstra can take a taxi. We'll have a drop of brandy and discuss what we should do tomorrow."

"Sir," de Gier said and got back in the car.

His mood improved when the commissaris raised his glass. The brandy smelled good, very good, and the commissaris was charming. He had apologized for keeping them so late and had flattered the two detectives by saying that he was enjoying working with them. He had gone to the kitchen and filled two bowls with chips and he had given Grijpstra the best chair in the room.

"Now," the commissaris said, "we don't seem to have achieved much tonight. It was clear that Mr. Wauters, our Belgian diplomat friend, wasn't prepared to tell us more than he had to. It was also clear that he didn't have an alibi."

De Gier took another sip and made the brandy roll on his tongue. He saw the noncommittal face of the diplomat again. The diplomat had been very polite. He had spent Saturday night in his bachelor flat, by himself. He had watched a little TV and gone to sleep early. He hadn't left his flat, he hadn't gone to Amsterdam, and he hadn't killed Mrs. van Buren.

"He admitted that Maria van Buren was his mistress," the commissaris said, "and he admitted that he paid her a monthly sum. He wouldn't say how much. He knew, he said, that she had other friends but he had always pretend-ed not to know. An arrangement between her and him.

Very convenient. Live and let live. Avoid costly confron-
tations. A true diplomat.''

"He didn't seem sorry she had died," de Gier said.

"Yes," the commissaris said, "that's an important
observation. I noted the same reaction when I saw the
American colonel this morning. The colonel was relieved,
and so was Mr. Wauters. They saw the woman regularly,
they went there to see her on their own accord, they spent
money on her, a lot of money in the colonel's case and
possibly also in the diplomat's case, but they were relieved to hear that they wouldn't have to go to see her
again."

"A witch," de Gier said.

"Beg pardon?" the commissaris asked.

"A witch, sir. She cultivated funny plants, we mentioned it in our report and the doctor confirmed that the
plants we found in her houseboat were poisonous. Belladonna and nightshade and something else, I forgot the
name."

"Ah yes," the commissaris said, "I saw the report.
Herbs. The third was thorn apple. Herbs are a craze
nowadays, everybody cultivates them. But people cultivate them for their kitchens and for medicinal purposes.
Nobody would cultivate poisonous plants."

"Mrs. van Buren did," Grijpstra said.

"You are suggesting that she was brewing poisons?"
the commissaris said, looking at de Gier, "brews which
she made her victims drink and which paralyzed their will
power in some way so that they were forced to come back
to her?"

De Gier didn't answer.

"Could be," the commissaris said. "Maybe she cast a
spell on them. Perhaps the spell consisted of her own
sexual power and whatever she made them drink or eat or
smoke. Or perhaps she burned a powder and they inhaled
the poison. The one force would enhance the other and

they would only be satisfied if they got the two together. But it is far-fetched. It's romantic, of course.''

"De Gier is very romantic," Grijpstra said.

The commissaris chuckled and refilled their glasses. "Your health gentlemen." They drank.

"Nostalgic is the word," the commissaris said. "We are being taken back to the Middle Ages, the dark times when people lived in small communities in great forests. It's a time we have forgotten but it's still in the memory of the people, hidden, but alive. Lately it is coming up again, I have seen it in the hippies. Some of them must look exactly like wizards' disciples, pure fourteenth century. Do you ever go to bookshops?''

"No, sir," Grijpstra said, "not very often."

"Yes, sir," de Gier said.

"You must have noticed that books on herbs are very popular. I have read some of them. Collected rubbish I would say, stuff you can find in the encyclopedia, but then bunched together and with a couple of drawings thrown in. The real books are not for sale. The old hermits had books but you could only use them if the hermit was prepared to train you, and you had to live with him for years and he would really teach you about plants. One could also find out by oneself I daresay, by trying to grow herbs and by studying them. I spend some time in my garden every day, it's amazing what you can learn. Do you have a garden?''

"I have some plants on my balcony, sir," de Gier said.

"What do you have?" the commissaris asked, looking very interested.

"Geraniums," de Gier said, "and something called asylum, a small plant with lots of little white flowers, it smells of honey."

"Alyssum," the commissaris said. "Do you ever look at your plants?''

"Yes, sir."

"And what do you see?''

"They are beautiful."

"Yes," the commissaris said slowly. "They are beautiful. Even geraniums are beautiful, almost everybody has them and they are beautiful. It's thc first lesson to learn."

He had spoken with some emotion and the silence had come back into the room. It was a pleasant silence and Grijpstra suddenly felt very peaceful. De Gier was sitting on the edge of his chair, the brandy glass in his hand, waiting for the commissaris to speak.

"But I am not prepared to believe that Mrs. van Buren was a witch. She may have had the plants for some other reason. Maybe she liked the look of them. She had lots of other plants as well. She had the colonel in her power and I am sure she had our Mr. Wauters under her spell. But she was a beautiful sexy woman. Women have power, a passive power. All they have to do is smile a little and men run to them. Men don't want to be manipulated but they are, by women and their own uncontrolled desires. Perhaps the colonel and Mr. Wauters are pleased now, because they can go and hunt for fresh game. And perhaps she was blackmailing them. Our friends wouldn't admit that they were being blackmailed. That's understandable. The blackmailer is dead and the secret has gone with her. Three detectives have gone through the houseboat today; tomorrow morning we'll know what they have found. Nobody has taken anything out of the ship for I had it guarded all night and this morning until the detectives arrived. Perhaps we'll find something."

"What did you think of the colonel, sir?" Grijpstra asked.

"An intelligent man," the commissaris said. "He admitted a lot which was good strategy if he had anything to hide. He even admitted having spent a fortune on her during the last three years, but a fortune he could afford to spend. Colonels have a good income, especially in the American army. He has an alibi and I am sure it's a good alibi. The American military police will be checking it now but it will hold. But the colonel said something which may support your theory, de Gier.''

''Did he say she was a witch?'' de Gier asked.

The commissaris smiled. ''No. But he said that she was very attractive and that I would have been interested in her if I had ever met her. I said that I am an old man and suffering from rheumatism. And then he said that Mrs. van Buren would perhaps have cured me. Rheumatism is hard to cure.''

''Did you ask him if Mrs. van Buren had been interested in plants?'' de Gier asked.

''No,'' the commissaris said. ''I didn't think of it. The remark only sunk in later.''

''You can contact the American military police and they can ask him,'' Grijpstra said.

''I may. And I may not.''

''You don't think it matters?'' de Gier asked.

''Perhaps not. She was killed by a man who didn't like her. He didn't like her because she was blackmailing him, or because she had humiliated him. She may also have been killed because she knew something. The Secret Service *is* interested in her and has been interested for some time. Perhaps some professional killer paid by an embassy has thrown the dagger. The fact that she is a witch, which isn't a fact so far, may have nothing to do with her death. We may have to consider her sorcery as a hobby.''

The commissaris got up. ''It's late, gentlemen, and you will want to go to bed. Tomorrow is another day and we'll see what it brings. I'll get hold of IJsbrand Drachtsma and make an appointment with him for the afternoon. You should be there as well and we can ask all the questions we want to ask without military policemen and diplomats hovering around us. Phone me at one o'clock tomorrow and I'll tell you when he is coming. Tomorrow morning you should try and find the man with the Edam cheese face, the fellow who wears a red waistcoat and who has a small son who plays with a ball. You can ask everybody in the area and show your sketch. While ~you find the red waistcoat I'll be contacting the police in Curaçao and find out as much as I can about Maria van Buren's background. Good night.''

"Sleep well, sir," de Gier said.

"Wait," the commissaris said. "I still have to phone a taxi for Grijpstra."

"It's all right, sir," Grijpstra said. "I'll walk to the taxi stand; it's a nice evening."

"As you wish."

The commissaris walked them to his front door and smiled as he shook hands. He looked very friendly.

"I hope that Belgian fellow hasn't done it," de Gier said when they were walking toward the taxi stand.

"Why not?"

"Because he is a diplomat, we can't arrest him."

"You want to punish somebody?" Grijpstra asked. "I thought you didn't believe in punishment. Didn't you tell me the other day that it would be much more fun catching criminals if you could be sure they would be taken to a nice place with a large park where they could relax and eat good food and play games and become healthy again?"

"Yes," de Gier said. "Criminals are sick people and should be cured in pleasant surroundings. But there are exceptions. This murderer killed a beautiful woman and beautiful women are scarce. A man like that should wear a ball and chain. And Mrs. van Buren was a witch as well. I would have liked to meet her."

"Ach," Grijpstra said.

"You don't agree?"

"I agree," Grijpstra said, and patted de Gier on the back. "Now you go home and go to sleep and dream dreams."

"Life *is* a dream," de Gier said.
"That's enough. Good night."
The taxi door slammed and the car took off.
De Gier waved.
Grijpstra didn't look around.

6

It was ten o'clock in the morning and it was raining. De Gier had just knocked on the door of a houseboat and was waiting for the door to open. He had put up the collar of his stylish raincoat and was muttering a string of curses, directed at himself who had bought the raincoat and the manufacturer of the raincoat who had forgotten to water-proof it.

The door opened and a fat woman, dressed in a torn peignoir and with her hair hanging down her face, looked at him with bleary eyes. "No, thank you," she said, and slammed the door.

De Gier knocked again.

"Go away," the woman shouted from inside the boat, "whatever it is you want to sell me, I don't want it."

De Gier knocked again.

"Go away," the woman shrieked, "or I'll phone the police."

"I *am* the police," de Gier shouted.

The door opened.

"Show your identification," the woman said, and pulled the card out of his hands. She studied the card, holding it at arm's length, spelling out the words to herself. "Amsterdam Municipal Police, R. de Gier, sergeant."

"All right," she said, "what do you want, sergeant?"

"Can I come in a minute?"

The woman stepped aside. De Gier gave her a photocopy of the sketch Bart de Jong had made of the man in the red waistcoat and his little son, holding a ball.

"Do you know this man at all, madam?"

"Let me get my glasses."

The fat woman got her glasses, polished them, and put them on. She studied the sketch carefully. "I have seen him," she said, "he only comes on Sundays, Sunday mornings. Walks about with his son. A lot of people come here for walks but I wouldn't remember them but I remember this one because of his silly waistcoat. A red waistcoat. He has a golden watch chain as well. He reminded me of my grandfather, that's why I remember him too."

"Do you know his name?"

"No," the woman said, "why should I? I never talked to him. Why are you looking for him?"

"We want to ask him a few questions," de Gier said, looking around and noticing how well kept the interior of the boat was. Everything was in its place, the furniture looked as if it had been polished a few minutes ago, the windows were so clean that he had to look again to make sure that there was glass in them. "Typical," de Gier thought, forcing himself to look at the woman who was still eyeing him suspiciously. "Ugly woman," de Gier thought, "should go on a diet and spend an hour a day on herself. She can't be thirty yet, could be quite attractive if she tried."

"Nice boat you have, madam," he said sweetly, "must be wonderful living out here on the water."

"I would prefer a nice apartment," the woman said, but she smiled.

"You didn't notice whether the man used to come here in a car and park it somewhere around here?"

The woman thought; the effort made her less ugly. "Yes. He might have come in a car. It's a long walk from the city and he had the little boy with him. Maybe he parked somewhere close by and then went for a walk. But I haven't seen his car."

"Thank you," de Gier said.

"Would you like some coffee, sergeant?"

"No, thank you, madam, I still have a lot of work to do."

De Gier left. It was the seventeenth door he had knocked on that morning. He knocked on another ten doors and finally got an answer. He walked back to the police VW where he found Grijpstra waiting for him, patiently smoking a cigar.

"What kept you?" Grijpstra said. "I have been waiting here for nearly half an hour. I looked for you, did you find a pretty lady somewhere?"

De Gier took a deep breath. "No."

"The man used to drive out here," Grijpstra said, "in a red Rover. I wanted to tell you."

De Gier took another deep breath. He had been training himself in mental discipline lately and had set himself several goals, such as not to smoke before breakfast, not to swear, to stop at orange traffic lights, to be modest. But the exercises were difficult and he didn't win much. He lost now.

"I know," he said.

"What do you mean you know?" Grijpstra asked gruffly.

"The man drove a red Rover."

"So why didn't you tell me?" Grijpstra asked. "I was running around knocking on doors and seeing a lot of old

women with curlers in their hair and you knew all the time.
What kept you?''

"Nothing kept me," de Gier said. "I was working and I
know more than your red Rover. Two girls live in a
houseboat right at the end, students. One girl studies
English and the other medicine.''

"Yes. And they were under the shower and you had to
dry their backs and then they made you some coffee and it
was rude to refuse. I know.''

"You know nothing," de Gier shouted. "*They* knew
something. They had seen the car and they remembered
the letters on the license plate.''

"So?''

"V.D.," de Gier said.

Grijpstra got out of the car and slapped de Gier on the
shoulder. "Splendid. Good work. Excellent. That's
enough for the clerks at Headquarters. You found our
man.''

De Gier had his first kind thoughts of the day and
thanked his fate. He knew other adjutants. He also thanked
the commissaris. The commissaris had made him Grijpstra's assistant.

"I am soaked," Grijpstra said, "and so are you. Let's
get back but let's go to your flat first and I'll have coffee
while you change your clothes and then we can go to my
house a minute so that I can change as well, and we'll
phone the commissaris from there.''

"Right," de Gier said.

"Yes," the commissaris said through Grijpstra's
phone. "IJsbrand Drachtsma is coming at two o'clock,
but I would like you to come to my office at one. The
detectives have finished their search in Mrs. van Buren's
houseboat and I would like to discuss their report with
you.''

The detectives had lunch in a cheap little restaurant
close to Headquarters. They ate quickly and rushed, still
chewing their last roll, to a room on the top floor of the

police building where two men in shirt sleeves were playing cards.

"Would you likc to do a little work?" de Gier asked politely.

"No," the men said.

"Good. A red Rover, new model. The license plate starts with the letters VD, we don't know the number. Who owns it?"

"An interesting question," one of the men said.

"How long will it take you?"

"A couple of minutes or a couple of hours, depends how lucky we are. It isn't urgent, is it?"

"It isn't urgent at all," de Gier said, "but I would like to have the man's name and address within ten minutes and while you are about it you might check if he has a record."

The men stopped playing cards.

"Ha," the commissaris said, "there you are. Did you find the man in the red waistcoat?"

"We know who he is, sir," Grijpstra said. "His name is Holman and he lives in town. He is the owner of a small firm specializing in the nut trade."

"Nuts?"

"Cashew nuts, walnuts, peanuts, any type of nuts. He imports them and resells them to the wholesalers and supermarkets and so on. We telephoned his office and made an appointment for five o'clock this afternoon; he is coming here, to our office. He sounded very upset."

"Did you tell him why you wanted to see him?"

"No, sir."

"Good," the commissaris said, and rummaged through the papers on his desk. "I have the report here on the search of the houseboat. The detectives told me all about it this morning but it is nice to have some facts on paper. Sit down and I'll tell you what we found out."

The detectives sat down and relaxed. De Gier was

rubbing his hands. The case was going well, he thought. The suspects were coming in, one by one. They were getting somewhere, but in the back of his mind a little thought was bothering him. He found the little thought and identified it. What if the killer was hired? He had never come across a hired killer before. Hired killers are professional. They have no real motive, they work for a fixed sum of money which will arrive in an envelope when the job is done. They have no personal connection with the victim. They are cool, disinterested. They only pay one visit to the victim's house. How long does it take to throw a knife? And how does a policeman catch a man who leaves no traces? The killer might even be a foreigner, especially flown in for the purpose of finishing Mrs. van Buren's life. He would have been shown the houseboat and a photograph and given a date and a time.

"You look worried," the commissaris said.

De Gier told the commissaris about his little thought.

"Yes," the commissaris said, "it worries me too. Very few people can throw a knife. In the army only special troops are taught to fight with knives. But perhaps the knife wasn't thrown, the doctor wasn't sure. But we shouldn't worry; worry is a waste of time. The woman was killed and somebody killed her. We have certain rules to follow in our investigation, and we are following the rules. We are interviewing the suspects. One of them may give us a clue. And we have searched the boat. Most of the information the detectives gave me this morning is negative. No fingerprints, the handle of the front door was wiped clean on the inside and outside, there were no signs of breaking-in so the visitor has let himself in with a key or Mrs. van Buren opened the door for him. The windows of the boat were closed except for two very small windows which must have been left open by Mrs. van Buren for ventilation. There is no way of entering through the small windows. The railing of the staircase was also wiped clean so the killer wasn't wearing gloves. The detectives found a metal strongbox in the bookcase which was locked. I had it opened and there was over a thousand guilders in cash in it. I have also been given a file with accounts and she had nearly thirty thousand guilders in her bank account. She has been paying taxes on a yearly income of twenty-five thousand guilders, her source of income is described as 'entertainment.' The houseboat is Mr. Drachtsma's property and she wasn't paying rent."

"Well," Grijpstra said, "that's not too bad. We know something anyway."

"There's a little more," the commissaris said. "I asked the detectives to look at her bookcase; I am always interested in what people read. She had a lot of books in Dutch, all novels by well-known writers. They wrote down the titles of the foreign books for me, must have taken them an hour at least. Perhaps de Gier was right, there were two shelves of books on witchcraft and sorcery, in five languages. She could read English, French and German but also Spanish."

"Curaçao is close to South America," de Gier said.

"Quite. There is one more item of interest. Look at this."

The commissaris produced two objects and put them on his desk. "What do you think these are?"

"Roots," Grijpstra said.

De Gier was looking at the roots with amazement. The roots were some fifteen centimeters long and looked like dried-out little men with spindly legs and complete with long thin penises. The little men had proper faces with noses and eyes.

"They look like little men," he said.

"They do, don't they? They are mandrake roots."

De Gier looked up. "Commissaris," he said in a low voice. "These things look evil; they are used in sorcery, aren't they?"

"They are. I asked the doctor to look at them and he recognized them at once. He told me a strange story. The plant these roots are part of is considered to be the most powerful sorcery-weed known. In the Middle Ages the weed was often found at the foot of a gallows, and it was said that they wouldn't grow from a seed but originated from the sperms ejected by criminals hanged at the gallows as they went into their final struggle with death."

"Bah," Grijpstra said.

The commissaris gazed at the adjutant. "You have been in the police a long time, Grijpstra, you should be used to this sort of talk. The traces we find often come from the human body. It's like the songs small children sing. 'Shit and piss. And blood, and sperms and slime and vomit and puss and snot and sweat.' "

"Yes," Grijpstra said. "Sorry, sir."

"Never mind. And you are right of course. The picture I was painting isn't very nice, but anyway that's how the plant was supposed to be born. And the sorcerers always went for the roots. The roots are so powerful that a man cannot dig them up without risking his life. As you can see the roots look human, and they *are* human, the sorcerers say. When you pull the root out of the ground it will utter a fierce yell and the yell may drive you crazy or kill you outright so the sorcerers would dig very carefully and attach a piece of string to the root and tie the other end of the string to the leg of a dog. Then they stopped up their ears with wax and called the dog and the root popped out of the ground."

De Gier was still studying the roots. He hadn't touched them but had bent down to get a close view.

"And what are the roots supposed to do?" he asked.

"The doctor wasn't sure. He thinks that they were worn around the neck as a talisman, giving the sorcerer special powers, but they can also be ground up and mixed with other weeds and dried mushrooms. I suppose one could make a brew out of them."

"It seems the lady *was* a witch," Grijpstra said, shaking his head. "I thought they had gone out of fashion."

The commissaris was going to say something but the telephone rang and he picked it up.

"Show Mr. Drachtsma in," he said. As he put the phone down he quickly swept up the roots and put them into the drawer of his desk.

IJsbrand Drachtsma had sat down in the indicated chair and was looking at the commissaris. He seemed enveloped in an imperturbable silence, built around him the way an egg envelops and protects the chick. De Gier was admiring this newcomer in the intimate circle of suspects. Drachtsma, de Gier was thinking, had to be an unusual man. He had been described as a tycoon, a leader. Drachtsma was chairman of a number of well-known companies. He would be very rich. He would also be very powerful, more powerful perhaps than a minister of state. Companies led by men like Drachtsma employ thousands of people. Whole fleets of merchant vessels move about the oceans because men like Drachtsma have picked up a telephone. The advertising companies which they own tell us what to buy and do; they shape the routine of our lives.

But, de Gier was thinking happily, if we simple policemen pick up a phone men like Drachtsma come to see *us*. We manipulate the manipulator.

"Glad you could come," the commissaris was saying. IJsbrand Drachtsma inclined his bald head slightly to acknowledge the remark. De Gier knew that Drachtsma was nearly sixty years old but the body sitting so close to him now radiated more energy than its age should allow for. Drachtsma's pale blue eyes had an eager glint in them as if this interview was a new experience he was planning to enjoy.

Drachtsma had taken a cigar out of the box on the table in response to the commissaris' hospitable suggestion and his strong suntanned hands were lighting it now, using a solid-looking gold lighter. His movements were sparse as if he was controlling his activity. The lighter burst into flame at the first flick. De Gier thought of his own lighter, which never worked properly and had to be coaxed to come to life in a different way each time.

"Just a few questions," the commissaris was saying and, "we won't detain you any longer than we have to," and Drachtsma had inclined his bald head again. The thin fringe which framed the polished skull hadn't gone altogether gray yet.

"Last Saturday night," Drachtsma answered in a deep voice, reverbating in his wide chest, "I was with my wife, on Schiermonnikoog. I often spend the weekends on the island. We had guests, business friends from Germany. I took them sailing during the afternoon and we listened to music during the evening. I'll give you their names and addresses if you like."

"Please," the commissaris said.

Drachtsma scribbled on a page of his notebook, a leather-bound notebook which came from his inside pocket. He tore out the page and gave it to the commissaris.

"Would you mind telling us what your relationship with Mrs. van Buren was?" the commissaris asked.

"She was my mistress."

"I see. I wonder if you could give us some details about the lady's life. Somebody killed her and he must have had a good reason. If we know who the lady was we may know who killed her."

"Yes," Drachtsma said. "I would also like to know who killed her. She didn't suffer, did she?"

"I don't think so. She was killed from the back and the knife went right in. She probably died immediately without knowing what had happened to her."

"Good," Drachtsma said.

The three policemen were watching him.

"Please tell us," the commissaris said.

"Ah. I am sorry. I was thinking about Maria. What can I tell you? I knew her when she was still married, her husband runs a textile plant which is part of the organiza-

tion I work for. I met her at a party and I think I fell in love
with her. She had her own boat and we would meet on the
lakes. She got a divorce."

"I am sorry," the commissaris said, "but I will have to
ask personal questions. I hope you don't mind the presence of my two assistants. They are charged with the
investigation of this murder and I like them to be part of its
various stages."

"That's all right," Drachtsma said, and smiled at the
two detectives. The smile was pleasant. Drachtsma knew
how to handle the lower echelons.

"Why didn't you marry Maria van Buren?" the commissaris asked.

"I didn't want to marry her," Drachtsma said, "besides, I was married already. I have a son and a daughter
and they are very fond of their mother. I am fond of their
mother myself. And, I don't think Maria would have
married *me*. She liked her privacy. I bought a houseboat
for her because she liked being on the water. At that time
her boat was the only one in that part of the Schinkel River.
There are a lot of boats around her now and I often
suggested that she should move but she got used to living
there."

"If she was your mistress living on your boat I presume
that you were sending her a monthly check."

"I was," Drachtsma said.

"Did you know that she had other lovers?"

"Yes. I didn't mind. I always telephoned before I came
to see her and she would telephone me at my office."

"I hope you don't mind my saying so," the commissaris said gently, "but you don't seem upset at her
death."

There was no answer.

"You don't mind that she is dead?"

"It is a fact now, isn't it?" Drachtsma asked. "I can't
change it. Everything comes to an end."

The blunt statement took some wind out of the commissaris' sails and it was a little while before the conversation found its course again.

"The knife," the commissaris said, "worries me. I have it here, let me show it to you."

Drachtsma handled the knife. "A fighting knife," he said thoughtfully.

"Do you know what sort of a knife it is?" Grijpstra asked suddenly.

Drachtsma turned and looked Grijpstra in the eyes. "Yes," he said, "it is a British commando knife."

"Very few people would know how to throw such a knife, I think," the commissaris said hesitantly.

"I think I can throw it," Drachtsma said. "We were trained with knives like this during the war. I had one when I landed in France and I killed a German with it."

"Would you know anyone who knew Mrs. van Buren and who could throw a knife like that?"

"No," Drachtsma said. "With the exception of myself," he added almost immediately.

"Would you know anyone who wanted her dead?"

"No," Drachtsma said again. "I don't think she had any enemies, and her lovers weren't jealous. I think she had only three, including myself, and one of them I know personally, an American colonel called Stewart. The other man is a Belgian. I have met him at a party but only for a few seconds; he seemed a very careful polished type, not at all the sort of man who would throw a knife into a woman's back."

"We have already questioned the two gentlemen," the commissaris said.

"I suppose they both have alibis?"

The commissaris ignored the question. "Just one more thing, Mr. Drachtsma," he said, "would you mind telling us how much you paid Mrs. van Buren?"

"Twenty-five thousand a year," Drachtsma said. "I was going to pay her a little more because of inflation. She never asked for money."

"Any extras?"

"Yes, I have bought her some jewelry and clothes and twice a year I would give her a ticket to Curaçao. Her parents live near Willemstad."

"Did you ever go with her?"

"I have little time," Drachtsma said. "The only island I really like is Schiermonnikoog."

"Thank you," the commissáris said, and briskly rubbed his hands. "The final questions: we found that Mrs. van Buren was interested in plants and herbs. I wonder if . . ." He didn't finish the question.

"Plants," Drachtsma said, and began to laugh. "Yes, I know about her plants. She always took me to special little shops where medicinal herbs are sold and she used to read a lot about her weeds as well. It was a source of irritation to me for often she would talk about herbs all night, and I didn't visit her to hear about herbs. We had a few fights about it and I have threatened to leave her if she wouldn't give up her silly witchcraft, but it was an empty statement, I don't think she would have cared if I had left her. She was a strong woman."

"A strong woman who got killed," the commissaris said. "Thank you, Mr. Drachtsma, I hope we won't have to bother you again."

"I don't think anybody could rattle *him*," Grijpstra said after Mr. Drachtsma had left.

"We'll see," the commissaris said quietly. "He is a Frisian, and Frisians have strong heads. And he isn't the only Frisian in the world. Weren't you born in the North, Grijpstra?"

"I was, sir, in Harlingen."

"I was born in Franeker," the commissaris said.

"One should never underestimate the provincials," de Gier said.

7

"Go on, hit him!" Grijpstra said.

De Gier stepped back, coolly eyed his opponent, and hit him. He rubbed his hand while the coffee machine obediently released a paper cup which had got stuck somewhere in its mysterious insides and filled it with a foaming thick liquid.

"Now it hasn't got enough water," Grijpstra said disgustedly. "Why can't we have a proper canteen like the one we used to have, with a nice elderly sergeant behind the bar who would forget to ask you for money sometimes?"

"We have run out of nice elderly sergeants," de Gier said. Grijpstra poured the contents of his paper cup into the plastic waste basket and began to look through his pockets.

"I have run out of cigarettes."

"There's another machine," de Gier said. "Put two guilders into it and push the button of your choice."

Grijpstra snarled at the machine. "No," he said. "I did it yesterday and it ate my two guilders and gave me nothing."

"You should have looked for the man; he has a key."

"The man," Grijpstra said. "What man?"

"The little fellow with the goat beard and the gray dustcoat. He is always scuttling about in the corridors."

"Not when *I* need him. I am going out to the shop. What shall we do while we wait for our friend Holman? We have more than an hour."

De Gier was combing his curls and observing his face in a mirror. He didn't answer.

"Beautiful man," Grijpstra said. "I am talking to you. In fact I am asking you a question."

"More than an hour," de Gier repeated, "an hour full of opportunities. An hour which we can use for some real purpose. An hour which is part of today, the most wonderful day of our lives."

"Yes," Grijpstra said. "An hour. What shall we do with it?"

"Have a cigarette," de Gier said.

"Thank you." Grijpstra lit the cigarette, inhaled, and managed a smile. De Gier put his comb back and adjusted his scarf.

"Let's go to my flat," de Gier said. "We can take the car. It'll only take ten minutes. I'll make you some real coffee and put on a record I bought at a sale last week for three guilders. A man playing church music on a recorder."

"Modern church music?" Grijpstra asked. "With drums in it?"

"No," de Gier said.

Grijpstra considered the proposition. He shook his head.

"No," he said, "there isn't enough time. Some other day perhaps. I don't mind listening to church music but if we have to rush out there and rush back we won't have a chance to concentrate. Good music needs concentration. Besides, your cat will get at me again. He got me this morning while you were having your shower. You should give that cat away, you know."

De Gier jumped as if he had been stung. "Why don't you give your wife away?" he asked in a sudden loud voice.

"Nobody wants her," Grijpstra said. "But somebody will want your cat. He is a beautiful animal, I'll say that for him, but I would have loved to wring his splendid neck this morning. You know what he did?"

"I hope he scratched you," de Gier said.

"No. He is more subtle than that. He did a number of things. First he jumped on my lap and growled a little. He has got a lot of teeth and a lot of claws and I didn't know what the growl meant so I just waited. Then he put his snout into my armpit and sniffed. He sniffed for half a minute. It was a very funny feeling."

"Ha," de Gier said. "You were wondering what it would be like to be bitten in the armpit?"

"Exactly. I am sure Oliver wanted me to wonder about that. He likes to create a sensation. Why did you call him Oliver?"

"That's his name," de Gier said. "Oliver Kwong. He is a pedigreed cat. His father came from the Far East."

"Kwong," Grijpstra said. "I might have known. I suppose old Kwong was owned by a mountain chief who would boil people alive if they didn't kneel down in his presence."

"Go on," de Gier said. "What else did he do?"

"He finally finished sniffing and climbed on my shoulder. Then he jumped into your bookcase and disappeared so I forgot about him until a lot of books dropped on my head."

"Yes," de Gier said, "he does that. He wrings himself through a small hole somewhere and gets behind the books. Then he stretches out to his full length and shoves. He can move as many as twenty books in one shove. He does it to me too and then he looks down and grins."

"You should hit him when he does that."

"No," de Gier said. "I never hit him. I think he is an intelligent cat. I have never heard of cats shoving books onto people. Did he do anything else?"

"Yes," Grijpstra said. "He jumped on that antique cupboard you have and stalked about for a while, pretending he was a tiger, but he annoyed me so I suddenly clapped my hands and yelled and he got a fright and forgot his act. Haha, you should have seen him, he tried to jump in two directions at once and fell off the cupboard. He really fell and he looked bloody silly when he scrambled about on the floor."

"Frightening a poor little animal," de Gier said contemptuously.

"Yes," Grijpstra said. "I frightened him out of his royal wits. About time somebody did."

"He'll bite you next time," de Gier said.

"If he bites me," Grijpstra said solemnly, and patted the large automatic pistol attached to his belt, "I will shoot him right between the eyes."

"If you shoot him," de Gier said solemnly, and patted the small automatic pistol stuck into a shoulder holster, "I will shoot you, right through the heart."

"Yes," Grijpstra said, "let's do that. I hope Sietsema and Guerts will be sent to investigate."

"They'll never catch me," de Gier said.

"Of course they will catch you," Grijpstra said.

They had walked back to their office and were now sitting down, each behind his own gray steel desk.

"They wouldn't, you know," de Gier said.

"You have thought of some brilliant strategy of escape?"

"Yes," de Gier said.

"Would you tell me?"

"Why should I?"

"Because I am your friend," Grijpstra said sweetly.

De Gier nodded. "Yes, you are my friend. I don't believe in friendship because, as Mr. IJsbrand Drachtsma explained this afternoon, nothing lasts and everything comes to an end and is, therefore, illusionary and without any real substance. But, for the time being anyway, you are my friend."

"So tell me how we wouldn't catch you."

"You would be dead," de Gier said.

"Ah true. How Sietsema and Geurts wouldn't catch you."

"Because I know how the city computer works. I would put on a white coat and mix with the other white coats and press a few buttons and I would have a new name. And then I would hire another flat. And then I would get a job as a trashman and the city would give me one of those clever motorized carrier cycles and a broom and I would be out in the sun all day and loaf a lot and talk to people and I would be happy."

"And we would never spot you?"

"You would be dead," de Gier said reproachfully.

"I keep forgetting. So the police would never spot you?"

"Never," de Gier said.

"They probably wouldn't," Grijpstra said. "Good idea. Thank you."

"You are going to try it out?" de Gier asked.

Grijpstra had picked up his drumsticks and sounded a hesitant roll.

"Good," de Gier said, and took out his flute. They played until the telephone rang.

"Mr. Holman has arrived," Grijpstra said, softly hitting the side of his drum. "The commissaris is waiting for us; he had him taken to his own room."

"What's all this?" de Gier asked. "I thought *we* were supposed to work on this case."

"Allow an old man his pleasure," Grijpstra said.

* * *

Mr. Holman's hand was flabby and moist but he tried to put some power in his grip. He was putting on a brave show. The commissaris had placed his guest in a low chair and the three policemen were looking down at their victim, who squirmed.

Grijpstra felt sorry for the fat man. He sat down himself and smiled.

Mr. Holman smiled back; the smile hovered on his thick lips, disappearing as soon as it had come.

"I read about Mrs. van Buren's death in the newspaper," he said in a high voice. "I was very sorry to learn that she was killed. She was a nice lady."

De Gier remembered that he had read Mr. Holman's file that morning. Two convictions. One for embezzlement some ten years ago, and one for causing grievous injuries. He had also studied the details of the two cases. Mr. Holman had, when he still worked for a boss, failed to hand in a few thousand guilders which a customer had paid for goods received. There had been no invoice but Mr. Holman had signed a receipt. Three months in jail of which two were suspended. And a year later he had hit his neighbor's son. The boy had been trampling on some young plants in Mr. Holman's garden. The boy had fallen against a fence post and had been taken to hospital. A slightly cracked skull. Three months in jail.

"A shifty violent character," de Gier thought but what he saw didn't agree with the conclusion he had drawn from the file. Like many fat men Mr. Holman looked jolly. "A jolly chap," the commissaris was thinking. "Pity he is so nervous."

Grijpstra was also thinking but vaguely. He had remembered that Mr. Holman sold nuts. Grijpstra liked nuts, especially cashew nuts which he sometimes bought in small tins. But the nuts were expensive. "If I were corrupt," Grijpstra thought, "I would make him give me a whole jute bag full of cashew nuts and I would go home and eat them."

"What was your relationship to Mrs. van Buren, Mr. Holman?" the commissaris asked.

"I just knew her," Mr. Holman said. There was a squeak in his voice which he tried to hide by clearing his throat.

"Tell us about it," the commissaris said pleasantly. "We are interested. She was killed as you know, murdered, and the more we know about her the easier it will be for us to find her killer. If she was a friend of yours you would want us to find her killer, wouldn't you?"

"Yes," Mr. Holman said, "yes, she was a friend of mine. But not a very good friend. It was all because of my little boy and his ball."

"Ball?" the commissaris asked.

"Yes. He dropped it into the Schinkel, into the river. He likes me to take him for a walk on Sunday mornings and we drive out to the Schinkel and park the car and then we walk. Sometimes we play with his ball. I don't like playing ball so usually he throws it about by himself, and one Sunday morning it went into the river. He is only four years old and he was very upset. I said I would buy him a new ball because it had floated out of reach but he began to howl so I knocked on Mrs. van Buren's door thinking I might reach the ball from her boat. I didn't know her then."

"And she asked you in?"

"Yes. She was very helpful."

"And did you get the ball?"

Mr. Holman suddenly giggled. "Yes, we got it in the end, but meanwhile my little son had managed to fall into the Schinkel. He fell out of the window."

"That must have been a nice morning," Grijpstra said, thinking of the many walks his children had forced him to make on Sunday mornings.

"A very complicated morning," Mr. Holman was saying. "We had to get his clothes off and dry them and I couldn't leave."

"Did you mind?" the commissaris asked.

"You have seen Mrs. van Buren, haven't you?" Mr. Holman asked.

"I saw her corpse, in the mortuary."

"I see. Well, she was very beautiful when she was alive."

"Did you get to know her well?" de Gier asked.

Mr. Holman was sweating. He took out a large handkerchief and dried his face. "No. Not the way you mean."

"How do you know what I mean?" de Gier asked.

"I know what you mean. But it wasn't like that at all. I just went to see her again and again. Always on Sunday mornings, and my little son was with me. She used to give me a cup of coffee and my son had his lemonade. We would stay half an hour maybe."

"You just talked?" the commissaris asked.

Mr. Holman was silent.

"No intimate relationship?"

"No sir."

The room was very quiet.

"Did your wife know about your meetings with Mrs. van Buren?"

Mr. Holman giggled again. "Yes. My son was always telling her about the nice lady. My wife wanted to go and meet the nice lady."

"Did she meet her?"

"No."

"She was killed on Saturday night," Grijpstra said.

"Saturday night," Mr. Holman said. "That's bad."

The policemen waited.

"I was in my office all Saturday afternoon and all Saturday evening. Only came home at eleven."

"Was there anyone with you at your office?"

"No," Mr. Holman said. "I was alone. I often work on Saturdays, best day of the week for me, no telephone, no visitors."

"Have you been in the army?" Grijpstra asked.

"No, I have a weak spine. Why?"

"I was just asking," Grijpstra said. "And you don't like sports, you were saying. You wouldn't play ball with your son."

Mr. Holman shook his head. "I am very fond of sports."

"Any particular sport?" the commissaris asked.

"Darts," Mr. Holman said. "I am good at darts. It isn't a popular sport in Holland but I like it. I have a special room in my house where we play. I am chairman of the society, you know."

"Darts is a throwing game," Grijpstra said slowly. "Can you throw this, you think?"

The stiletto gleamed in his hand; it had flicked open as he had pulled it out of his pocket.

"Sure," Mr. Holman said. "Where do you want me to throw it?"

"Into the cigar box," the commissaris said, "but wait a moment. I'll take the cigars out first."

The commissaris put the empty cigar box on a filing cabinet. "Right," he said.

Mr. Holman had got up and was balancing his feet. He half-closed his eyes, weighing the knife in his open hand. "There," he said.

The movement had been very quick. Grijpstra's stiletto had hit the cigar box squarely in the middle, and had pierced the flimsy wood. There wasn't much left of the box.

As Grijpstra began to walk toward the filing cabinet to retrieve his knife, Mr. Holman understood.

"The knife was thrown, wasn't it?" he asked in a whisper.

"It was," the commissaris said.

"I didn't kill her," Mr. Holman said, and began to cry.

* * *

The room was quiet again. Mr. Holman had left, loudly blowing his nose. He had been answering questions for more than an hour.

"Well?" the commissaris asked after a few minutes. Grijpstra and de Gier stared at him.

"Well?" the commissaris asked again.

"Difficult," Grijpstra said.

The commissaris chose a cigar from the disorderly heap on his desk.

"Must get a new cigar box," he muttered to himself, and aloud, "You shouldn't have that stiletto, Grijpstra."

"No, sir," Grijpstra said.

"No motive," de Gier said loudly. "No motive at all. Why should he want to kill a woman who gave him cups of coffee and who gave his little boy glasses of lemonade? He wasn't a client of hers and she couldn't have blackmailed him."

"Why not?" the commissaris asked.

"He wouldn't be visiting her on Sunday morning if she was playing whore for him during the week."

"Quite," Grijpstra said.

"Perhaps he didn't have to pay," the commissaris said. "Perhaps they were lovers."

"That meatball?" de Gier said.

"Women," the commissaris said in a lecturing voice, "are not mainly attracted by a man's looks."

De Gier looked hurt and Grijpstra looked amused.

"Maybe he gave her flowers," Grijpstra said, "and recited poetry and paid her compliments."

"All right," de Gier said. "He was her lover. He sang songs to her. And then he threw a knife into her back."

"We'll have to see him again," the commissaris said. "Phone him at his office tomorrow morning and ask him to be here at three in the afternoon."

He got up and opened the door.

* * *

"He is liking this case," Grijpstra said as they walked back to their room.

"I am not," de Gier said. "Are you?"

"Yes," Grijpstra said. "It's a nice case, nice and complicated. Let's go to a café and have a drink and go through it again. We have a lot of information now."

"No," de Gier said.

8

THE RAIN was thick and cold and thoroughly unpleasant but the commissaris, a dapper pedestrian in a black oil-cloth coat and a floppy hat, didn't mind. The only concern that his brain was registering was a concern about the pain in his legs. Rain aggravated his rheumatism and his limp was obvious that morning, in spite of his efforts. He was forcing himself to breathe slowly. Slow breathing improved his resistance. He was also forcing himself to think about something that had nothing to do with his pain. He was thinking about the Secret Service and his thoughts amused him so that his expression was a mixture of joy and suffering, resulting in an odd grimace. He wondered how many people knew that the Secret Service had a local head office that was separate from its three rooms at Police Headquarters, and he wondered if there would be any people who would care.

He had seen the chief constable that morning, to ask for an introduction to the director of the Secret Service. The introduction had been arranged within a few minutes. And

now he was on his way. He knew the address, had known
it for some years but there had never been a reason to
penetrate into this seat of mystery.

He stumbled on a cobblestone and supported himself
against the cast-iron railing of a bridge. He cursed, a long
full-blooded curse, venomously pronounced, each syllable stressed. The pain was now a little worse and he
waited until he had regulated his breathing again.

He wished he could have avoided this visit but had to
agree with himself that he couldn't have. The Secret
Service had alerted the police, an unignorable fact. They
had, in some so far unexplained way, discovered that Mrs.
Maria van Buren was not the simple lone woman living on
a houseboat she might have pretended to be.

The commissaris shook his head and grumbled. They
still didn't know much about the dead woman.

He had arrived and looked at the dilapidated narrow
gable house. He checked the number and smiled. He knew
the house. He smiled again. He knew the house well. He
had visited it several times, but long ago. Thirty-five years
ago, before the war it had been. The house had looked
better in those days. It had been a great house, quiet and
dignified, furnished with dark red velour drapes and thick
semitransparent lace and a wealth of Victorian furniture. It
had catered to the weird tastes of some of the richest men
of the capital. His suddenly activated memory produced a
series of fairly sharp color photographs. He remembered
the fat oily face of Madame and the luscious body of
Mimi, a Javanese girl who could only be rented for short
periods at an exorbitant rate for she was first choice. She
had her own large room on the second floor, a room full of
mirrors. The commissaris had spent several hours with the
mirrors, enervated by the reflection of his own body
shown from every possible angle. It had been on the day
that old Mr. de V. had been found in that room and old Mr.
de V. hadn't been a pretty sight with all the lights switched
on, looking rather bulbous, like an overgrown white

mushroom. He had died, of a stroke, but the doctor wasn't sure and the police were invited. The commissaris was an inspector at the time. An evening which made an impression on his inexperienced mind.

Madame dropped a heavy hint that evening and the hint had made him return, about a week later. Madame had been very good to him, giving him his choice of four ravishing girls and the use of the mirror room and she opened the bottle of champagne herself, with her pudgy bejeweled hands. He had paid for the second bottle himself but was only charged a quarter of the usual price.

The small oilcloth-covered figure on the steps of the old house straightened itself as the memories flooded its brain. A very memorable evening indeed. The girl was French, genuinely French and he had practiced his knowledge of the language on her and she had corrected his mistakes and giggled beautifully and done far more than he had expected her to do.

He had visited the house once more. A client, a foreigner fortunately, had, in a frenzy of rage and frustration, wounded a girl with a small fork. The wound wasn't serious but the client was arrested nevertheless. Client and girl had been eating small pieces of buttered toast, thickly covered with caviar, and the minute black eggs were mixed up with blood on the alabaster body of the girl. A horrible but also rather interesting sight. And now he was visiting the house again, for the fourth time. He rang the bell.

Would the present occupants know about the history of the house? They probably would not, the commissaris thought. As he waited for somebody to open the door he became more certain that they wouldn't know.

They didn't even know that he was ringing the bell. He rang again.

A slow shuffling sound approached and the door creaked open. An old man, in the city's uniform, the collar of his jacket decorated with the three crosses of the arms of

Amsterdam, faced the commissaris, although "faced" was, perhaps, an exaggeration. The old man didn't really have a face. The commissaris found himself confronted with a mask, made of old yellowed putty and, again, he was reminded of the brothel of a past now so far away that it seemed dated in the dream time, which also had an aged doorman who would stare at the customers as if he didn't know why they had taken the trouble of ringing the bell.

"I have an appointment with your director," the commissaris said, and the doorman forced his back into a slight bow, and stepped back.

Perhaps the old man was dumb but his attitude indicated servility and the commissaris felt grateful, his presence had been acknowledged.

The door closed behind him and he was led up a flight of stairs toward the mirror room. He tittered and half-expected his guide to stop and ask for an explanation but their slow procedure was uninterrupted and another door opened.

The mirrors had gone.

But some of the furniture was still there and the commissaris sat down on a chair upholstered in red velour, an old chair, a chair he had sat on before, but the mood had changed. He was neither breathless nor excited. Now, he dryly stated to himself, he was bored. No other word for it. Bored.

His host had helped him out of his coat and hung it on a heavy copper hook; his hat crowned the coat. He had shaken his host's hand and they had agreed on the weather. He also knew his host's name, and his rank. A naval commander. So that's what happened to the navy, he told himself. The ships are tied up in the river, and here is their last man, an old man, for the commander was old, close to retirement, like himself.

He noted, without any surprise, that his host's feet were covered by slippers, worn and shabby. He also noted that the commander's face reminded him of the face of a turtle, a dried-out face with patient eyes embedded in heavy folds. The commissaris liked turtles and kept one in his garden. He called it "Turtle" but it would never come when he called it by its name. He approved of his turtle's supreme indifference and fed it well, with fresh lettuce leaves, put out on the center of the small lawn of his garden, every night without fail.

"Yes," the turtle was saying now, "the van Buren case. Poor woman has been murdered, I hear."

"So she has," the commissaris agreed.

"Sad," the turtle replied.

"Very," the commissaris answered.

They didn't stare at each other. The turtle's look had turned inward and the commissaris had closed his eyes. His legs hurt him very badly now and all his energy was directed toward the rhythm of his breathing.

A clock ticked slowly on the wall. The door opened and closed. A pot of coffee, a sugar bowl, a jug of cream, and two cups and saucers had appeared on the turtle's desk, all dating back to the days of the brothel but the commissaris was no longer amused; he had accepted the fuse of past and present.

The turtle inhaled, waited, and began to speak.

"We would like to be of help."

The commissaris breathed, very quietly, counting to himself, up to four for inhaling, up to six for exhaling.

"But I am afraid there is little we can do."

The commissaris continued counting.

"You see, we don't know much."

The pain was under control now, and the commissaris fumbled in his pockets.

"A cigar?"

"Please."

The cigar was lit.

The turtle spoke without any prompting, eager to share his knowledge.

"Mrs. van Buren was friendly with several men. The

American intelligence people informed us about her possible importance; it seemed she had befriended an officer, an expert on atomic warfare. We were asked to keep her under observation."

"Yes," the commissaris said.

"But we get many requests like that and we don't always do as we are told."

"No."

"But then Brussels also pulled the bell. The same Mrs. van Buren had entered into a relationship with one of their men, a diplomat charged with security, security of the state."

"So you thought there was something in it," the commissaris said.

The turtle smiled. The commissaris didn't feel obliged to say anything.

"We don't think much," the turtle ventured.

"No."

"No," the turtle said. "We don't. But we do our job."

"So you contacted us."

"Yes," the turtle said.

The silence lasted and the commissaris got up. "That was all?" he asked, feeling that he was committed to make sure.

"Yes," the turtle said.

"It may be that Mrs. van Buren's death had nothing to do with secrets," the commissaris said feebly, feeling somewhat caught.

"It may be," the turtle said. "Have some more coffee before you go. The weather is still awful."

The commissaris emptied his second cup and shook hands. The turtle's hand felt as it should feel, dry and leathery.

The commissaris felt that he should ask the question. "Have you been here long? In this house I mean?"

"Ten years," the turtle said.

"Property of the state, is it?"

"Of course," the turtle said. "Why?"

"Just wondered. I wonder how she got it?"

"Bought it, I imagine," the turtle replied kindly.

The turtle had been right, the weather was still awful.
The commissaris rang the bell again and asked the doorman to phone for a taxi. He waited in the corridor but the
taxi didn't arrive.

"Never mind," he said in the end. "I suppose they are
busy, everybody wants a cab with this rain. Tell the driver,
if he does arrive, that I couldn't wait."

The doorman saluted and the door opened and closed
again.

"I am getting a lot of information," the commissaris
told himself as he walked back to Headquarters, "and all
of it is negative. We are getting nowhere."

The conclusion cheered him; he had been wishing for a
difficult case.

He thought of his time limit. The chief inspector would
be back within ten days. It would be awkward to have to
tell his assistant that a murderer was still wandering about.
But he shrugged the thought off. He would proceed as
dictated by the rules. No hurry. Hurry is a fundamental
error. Where did I get that? the commissaris asked himself. He remembered, he had got it from a Chinese story, a
wise story. He had begun to read books about ancient
China at about the same time that his rheumatism had
started to fire the nerves of his legs. "Pain and wisdom,"
he thought. "Perhaps there is some connection."

The idea occurred to him that perhaps he should be
grateful for his pain, it was leading him to discoveries,
but, as he slowly turned the next corner and began to
follow another canal, he rejected the conclusion. He
would rather have no wisdom and no pain. He walked for
another quarter of an hour thinking of the days when he
had no wisdom. He saw himself entering the brothel

again, on an evening in September of 1938, a young man, freshly bathed and filled with anticipation. The night of the room with the mirrors, the champagne, and the girl with the narrow hips and the full breasts.

"Morning, sir," a uniformed sergeant at Headquarters said. "How are you feeling this morning?"

"Fine," the commissaris said. "Lovely day."

"For frogs and officers," the sergeant said softly.

"Try the Curaçao police again," the commissaris said to the girl at the switchboard. "Chief Inspector da Silva in Willemstad."

Within ten minutes the phone rang.

The connection was bad and the commissaris had to shout a good deal. The chief inspector was very helpful. Yes, he had gone into the matter. Yes, Mrs. van Buren was a daughter of Mr. de Sousa of Curaçao. Yes, Mr. de Sousa was an important citizen. No, nothing was known on the island, nothing that could be a cause of Mrs. van Buren's untimely death in Amsterdam. Chief Inspector da Silva was sorry but that was all he could say.

The commissaris sighed and dialed a two-digit number. "The chief constable, please," he said politely.

He waited. "Morning, sir. The Secret Service knows nothing."

"It never does," the chief constable said.

"I think I should go to Curaçao."

There was a short silence and the commissaris found himself staring hard at his telephone.

"Well, if you think it is necessary."

9

"BUTTON UP your shirt," Grijpstra said. "I can see your undershirt. Your orange undershirt."

He sounded surprised.

"Have you never seen an orange undershirt?" de Gier asked.

"No. Don't want to either."

De Gier fumbled with his shirt.

"The button is gone," Grijpstra said, leaning closer. "Ha!"

"Ha what?"

"You are getting fat," Grijpstra said triumphantly.

De Gier jumped up and left the room. Grijpstra ran after him. He found de Gier staring at himself in the large mirror which had been placed in the corridor by a chief constable who wanted his men to look neat.

"Stand normally," Grijpstra said. "Breathe out! You'll choke if you breathe in only."

"Fat," de Gier said.

"A little fat," Grijpstra said. "It's your age. The mus-

cles go soft and gradually the stomach begins to pop out.
Don't worry."

"No."

"But it may get worse. I had an uncle who had a figure a
little like yours. He had to wear a corset in the end."

"What happened to your uncle?" de Gier asked.

"Oh, he died, why?"

"What age?"

"Forty-eight, forty-nine, I believe."

"What of?"

"Vanity," Grijpstra said. "Plain vanity. Looking in
the mirror. He got fatter and fatter and he kept on buying
stronger corsets and one day the veins in his neck burst.
But what do you care about my uncle? Did you read the
commissaris' note on my desk?"

"Yes," de Gier said. "I read all the notes on your desk.
He has gone to Curaçao and he won't be back for a few
days and we are to continue our investigations."

Grijpstra nodded.

"So what do you plan to do?"

"Follow me."

De Gier followed and they landed up near the coffee
machine where Grijpstra waited until de Gier had found
the right coins. The machine worked.

"I have followed you," de Gier said. "Now what?"

"I don't know," Grijpstra said. "We could telephone
Mr. Holman again and ask him to come to see us."

"We did that yesterday."

"And the day before yesterday."

"If he comes today he'll cry again."

"He hasn't done it," de Gier said.

Grijpstra leaned against the whitewashed wall and
sipped his coffee. "Why hasn't he done it? He has admitted that he has seen Mrs. van Buren by himself, hasn't
he? First he said that he always took his little son but later
he admitted that he has been to the houseboat by himself."

"On Sunday mornings only."

"So he says but why shouldn't he have made love to her on Sunday mornings. What's wrong with Sunday mornings?"

"That fat fellow?"

"Come off it," Grijpstra said. "He isn't so fat, no fatter than you will be in a few years' time. And he has a nice pleasant face. Perhaps he gave her a feeling of security. Perhaps she cuddled him. She could never have cuddled her paying lovers. The colonel, the diplomat, and our friend Drachtsma are all over six feet and wide-shouldered and dynamic and handsome. Perhaps she got tired of their profiles and muscles. So jolly Mr. Holman became her true lover. On Sunday mornings."

"Right," de Gier said. "Wonderful. Romantic. They had coffee or hot cocoa or milk with honey and nutmeg and they made warm cozy love to each other and then he bounced home again."

"Yes. But he got tired of her and she threatened to tell his wife so he sweated for a day or two and made up his mind and practiced with his darts. And then he found that lovely wicked knife in a second-hand store in the inner city and he took it home and threw it for an hour or so and then he went to see her last Saturday night and threw it right into her back. Swish. Plop."

"No," de Gier said.

"Why not? He is a violent man. Some little boy steps on a plant in his garden and he gives the little fellow such a wallop that he lands up in hospital with a cracked skull. And he is untrustworthy. His boss trusted him and he stole a couple of thousand guilders when he thought nobody was looking. You have read his file, haven't you?"

"I have read his file."

"So?"

De Gier walked over to the window and looked down into the courtyard where four stolen cars, found by the night patrol, were waiting for their rightful owners. He thoughtfully scratched his bottom.

"So?"

"Maybe. But I don't think so. Perhaps you are right. He is in a terrible state. Every time we ask him a question he wipes his face with that large handkerchief and he gets tears in his eyes and finally he cries. He hasn't got an alibi. But he threw that stiletto of yours into the commissaris' cigar box. That was really silly, wasn't it?"

"Yes," Grijpstra said, "that was silly. But we would have found out about his darts anyway. He knew we would, so perhaps it was very clever to play along with us."

"A lover and a genius," de Gier said.

"He deals in nuts, remember? He set himself up in business after he had been in jail twice. He runs his own business so well that he owns a nice house in a good area and a brand-new red Rover. A Rover is a pretty posh car. I have spoken to two of his clients pretending I wanted some information about his commercial reliability. They spoke very highly of him. He does all his own selling and buying and he has only one employee, an old spinster who answers his phone when he isn't there. I am convinced that he is an intelligent man; to build up a good business in a few years' time takes brains. And discipline."

"You think we should arrest him?"

"No," Grijpstra said, "we can only hold him for a few days. There is no evidence at all. We'll have to make him confess."

"Play cat and mouse? Make him come every day, and then give him a break, and then make him come every day again? Phone him at his house with odd questions?"

Grijpstra didn't answer.

"It's a nasty game, you know. Last time we did it the man had a nervous breakdown and his wife nearly divorced him and he was innocent."

"Yes," Grijpstra said, "I won't forget that case."

"To hell with it," de Gier said, and jumped up. "The boss is away and we have no real plans for today. Let's go."

"Where? It's raining."

"To my flat," de Gier said.

They got to the flat within a quarter of an hour and de Gier put on a record for Grijpstra and took Oliver with him into the kitchen. Oliver growled and scratched at the door.

"You can have him later. Let me make some pancakes."

"Pancakes," he said a little later. "You like pancakes. You can have them with ham, with honey, or with syrup. And this is good coffee. You can have a good cigar as well. Put your feet on that chair."

"Yes," Grijpstra said, "I'll do all that. Put jam on the pancakes. And watch your cat."

Oliver was growling in a corner and sharpening his nails on the carpet while he was fixing Grijpstra with his clear blue slanting eyes.

"Shit," Grijpstra said. "There must be something wrong with you that you like that cat."

"He is called Oliver. And he sleeps in my arm."

"Frrrooo," Grijpstra said softly.

He ate his pancakes, burped, and lit his cigar.

De Gier put on another record and together they listened to church music, an organ playing Bach. Oliver jumped on Grijpstra's lap, purred, and fell asleep. De Gier was stretched out on the floor, his head cradled in his arms. The record came to an end.

"Beautiful," Grijpstra said, and opened his eyes. He scratched Oliver behind the ears. The cat began to purr again.

"You see," de Gier said.

"Perhaps."

"If the commissaris thought Holman had done it he wouldn't have gone to Curaçao."

"No," Grijpstra said. "Curaçao is a warm island. The commissaris has an eternal pain in his legs. He wanted to warm his legs. He'll be on a deck chair somewhere now, on the terrace of a hotel. He took the opportunity when it presented itself. The case is stuck and the lady comes from Curaçao. He has to investigate her background. It takes only eight hours to fly there and the State is paying for his ticket."

"We can't solve the case while he is away," de Gier said, rolling over on his back, "it'll make him look silly."

"She didn't blackmail the diplomat."

"Why not?"

"She couldn't have. He isn't married."

De Gier sat up. "You are forgetting the Secret Service. They are in this too. She may have known secrets the diplomat shouldn't have told her about."

"Ha," Grijpstra said. "What secrets? Belgium isn't at war. They are like us. Belgium is a small comfortable country spending its time manufacturing things and selling them."

"Exactly. Commercial secrets or secrets involving the economy. Certain nations (he was dropping his voice) are very interested in ruining the economy of the Common Market. Diplomats always know too much and beautiful women are sent to lure them to their houseboats. The diplomats boast."

"No," Grijpstra interrupted, "not our diplomat. He wouldn't have wasted his time boasting. He went to her boat to sleep with her. He made her perform. He played with her or he made her play with him. And then he got into his clothes and into his black Citroën and he drove home."

"You don't suspect the diplomat?"

"No," Grijpstra said.

"The colonel?"

Grijpstra hesitated.

"No?"

"The colonel is separated from his wife. She lives in the States somewhere, he said. She'll probably know that he won't spend his nights by himself. Mrs. van Buren couldn't have blackmailed him that way."

"Atomic warheads," de Gier said.

"Yes. But we won't have to follow up on that. The military police are after him. And he has an alibi."

"He could have sent a killer, some paratrooper or ranger or special-service man or whatever they call their murderers. Americans kill each other at the drop of a hat."

De Gier laughed.

"The drop of a hat," Grijpstra repeated.

"Nobody wears hats anymore."

"They drop them."

"Not the colonel," de Gier said.

Grijpstra sighed. "You know we are getting close, don't you?" de Gier asked.

"Yes," Grijpstra said.

"IJsbrand Drachtsma," de Gier said in a firm voice.

"He has an alibi."

"So he says."

"The commissaris has checked it."

"So the commissaris says."

"You don't believe him?"

"Oh sure, I believe him. He spoke to the German businessmen Drachtsma had to his house that evening and they said they were there with him. There is no way of getting to Amsterdam from Schiermonnikoog unless you use the ferry, and the ferry only goes twice a day at this time of the year. Schiermonnikoog has no airport. But Drachtsma is a wealthy man."

"Ha," de Gier said. "A helicopter picked him up, on the beach. It dropped him on another beach where a fast car was waiting for him. He raced it to Amsterdam, let himself into the houseboat with a key, and swish and plop."

"Yes," Grijpstra said.

"Balls."

"Yes. There are nine hundred people to the square mile in Holland. The helicopter couldn't have picked him up without them seeing it. True, true. So he didn't do it."

"A pity," de Gier said, "because he is dangerous all right. The diplomat doesn't scare me and if the colonel was after me I would offer to buy him a drink but if IJsbrand Drachtsma . . ."

"You are serious?"

"I am," de Gier said. "He escaped to England in 1943 when the Germans were watching every inch of the beaches."

"And the engine of his rowboat broke down."

"Just imagine what it must have been like," de Gier said. "Twenty or thirty hours to go and the beaches looking at you with a thousand eyes. Nasty German eyes peeping out from under their heavy helmets, and machine guns and cannon everywhere and fighter planes in the sky and you sit there in your nutshell tinkering with an outboard engine and the others are rowing and dropping their oars and cursing."

"Would be fun," Grijpstra said.

"I always wanted to do it, but I was a little boy then. Where were you?"

"I spent the last year on a farm, working and trying to repair an old motorcycle. Took me all winter and then the war was over and it wouldn't go."

"Doesn't he scare you?" de Gier asked.

"No. I have nothing to lose. Besides, he irritates me. Cocksure, that's what he is. He has spent a lifetime winning."

"You haven't lost, have you?"

"No," Grijpstra said, "or perhaps I have. There isn't much difference. But *he* doesn't know. You remember the way he smiled to us when the commissaris introduced us as his assistants?"

"He smiled *down*."

"Of course he did. It looked friendly but it wasn't."

"He didn't kill her, because he wasn't there. He must have sent someone."

"But why would he have wanted her dead?"

"Blackmail," de Gier said. "What else? He is married and she was threatening to break up his marriage. Perhaps he has all his property in his wife's name. The house in Schiermonnikoog, the house in Amsterdam, his yacht, his airplane, the houseboat, his shares."

"We should meet his wife."

"There's something else," de Gier said, "something I haven't told you about."

"You should tell me everything," Grijpstra said.

"Yes, that young fellow, short, wears a brown imitation fur coat, looks like a musician."

"What about him?"

"I asked him to wait in the corridor when we were grilling Drachtsma, trying to grill him I should say for he was winning that time. I wanted to know how Drachtsma would behave after we had done with him. Cardozo hung about outside and when Drachtsma came out Cardozo was walking behind him, pretending he was going somewhere. They went to the main entrance downstairs together. The door is always locked and the constable who watches the door has a button which he has to press to release the lock. Drachtsma showed his slip, the constable pressed his button, and the door opened. It's a door you have to push."

"Yes, yes," Grijpstra said, "I know the door, I go through it a hundred times a day."

"Quite. But Drachtsma didn't push the door, he kicked it, with his great smelly boot, and as he went through it he farted. A nasty noisy smelly fart."

"And Cardozo got it right in the face?"

"He did."

"You shouldn't trust these young detectives, they tell you what you want to hear."

"No," said de Gier. "Cardozo is all right. He told me what he saw, and what he smelled in this case."

"Yes," Grijpstra said, "and Drachtsma's home is on Schiermonnikoog. Right?"

Grijpstra got up, forgetting Oliver who had to wake up suddenly and who dug his claws into Grijpstra's legs. Grijpstra yelled and Oliver hung on. Grijpstra backed into the bookcase and de Gier tried to help. A vase fell and broke on the floor splashing water on Oliver who had dropped to the ground. Oliver yelled and bit de Gier on the leg. It took a little while before the room became quiet again.

"He is a challenge," Grijpstra said, "keeps you on your toes. Every policeman should have a cat like that; I will suggest it to the chief constable. We'll be the most aware police force on earth."

"Yes. I am glad you appreciate him now. So we go to the island. When?"

"Tomorrow," Grijpstra said. "First boat tomorrow and we'll play it easy. It is a nice island; I have been there before, I even know the local chief of police. He is an adjutant and he likes birds. Let's be tourists and see what we can see. The commissaris is on an island too."

De Gier was putting his jacket on and looking at himself in the mirror. He was mumbling to himself.

"We still have the afternoon," Grijpstra said. "Go to the gymnasium and practice some judo. You have been getting lazy lately. You aren't as good as you used to be. I saw Geurts throw you twice in two minutes the other night. Geurts, of all people!"

"The instructor had asked me to let Geurts get some exercise," de Gier said.

"Sure."

"You don't believe me?"

"Sure."

"Listen here," de Gier said. "Half the fun of judo is to

let somebody else throw you. You learn to fall that way.
It's very important to be able to fall.''

"Sure," Grijpstra said.

"All right," de Gier said, "and what are you going to
do this afternoon?''

"I am going to fire thirty rounds at the range and then
I'll clean my pistol. And I'll ask the sergeant if I can fire
the carbine a few times and then I'll find someone who
knows about knife throwing. I'll throw a knife until I hit
something with it and then I'll go home.''

"I hope it will take you all night," de Gier said, and
dialed a number. "The boat leaves at ten A.M. tomorrow,''
he said, putting the phone down. "I'll pick you up at
seven.''

"No," Grijpstra said. "We can't take the car. There
are no cars allowed on the ferry and we may have to spend
a few days on the island. We'll take the train. I'll meet you
at the station at six-thirty.''

10

THE KLM PLANE began its descent toward Plesman Airport, Curaçao, and the commissaris woke up. His small wizened face looked almost eager and he acknowledged his own excitement with good-natured understanding. He hadn't traveled much in his life although he had wanted to, and apart from the south coast of France, where he had spent a number of holidays with his family, first in cheap hotels and later in a rented cottage, he only knew the world through books which he collected, buying them second-hand from the book stalls in the Old Man's Gate in the inner city. He had looked through the few books which mentioned Curaçao, immediately after he had come home to tell his wife that he was leaving the next morning, and while his wife fussed and packed his suitcase and found his passport and his medicines, he turned the pages of a thin volume written by a poet who had lived on the island. He read the lines aloud, repeating some of the words. "Cunucu," the commissaris said.

"Yes, dear?" his wife asked.

"Cunucu, that's the outback, the outback of Curaçao."

"Outback?" his wife asked.

"Fields," the commissaris said, "with nothing on it. Just cactuses, I imagine, and a few goats maybe. There used to be forests and Indians."

"Ah," his wife said, folding up a shirt. "Do you want a lot of ties?"

"Not too many. I wonder who chopped the forests down. I hope the Spanish did. They had it before us, you know."

"Indians?" his wife asked.

"There aren't any left."

"Where did they go?" his wife asked, tucking some socks into a corner of the suitcase.

"We must have murdered them. Or the Spanish did."

"Ah," his wife said.

"A land of grasshoppers and prophets," the commissaris read aloud. "I wonder what that means." He looked at his wife but she had stopped listening.

He was looking at the cunucu now, a dry brownish veld stretching on for miles, and he was pressing his nose against the little window. The thorned bushes and pale green cactus trees seemed thrown about haphazardly. A dreary land, but then he looked at the coastline and changed his mind. The sea was breaking against rough cliffs, sending up rhythmical spray in high sparkling waves, sun-drenched curtains, transparent and cool. "Lovely," the commissaris thought, rubbing his dry hands. "I must go out there. I'll hire a car and go by myself."

He saw the road, a narrow strip of tar, following the coastline. There were a few cars. The plane was low now and the view very clear. He saw an old Negro riding a donkey. He also saw the airport and a row of old-fashioned planes, bombers which he remembered having seen during the war. He recognized the Dutch markings on their gray sides. Dutch bombers on an island in the Caribbean. He shook his head. But he was still excited. There would be much to see, much to think about later, when he would be back in his garden in Amsterdam fighting the pain in his legs. Then he noticed that the pain had stopped. There was no pain at all, not even the slight twinge vibrating in his bones which had never left him during the last five years. The discovery stunned him. No pain. He saw himself living on this island, in a cottage, or even in an adobe hut like the one he had just seen on the cunucu. He would sit in the shadow of a tree and smoke a cigar and there would be no pain. But then the twinge returned and he shrugged.

"Silva," the big man with the suntanned face said as he carefully shook the commissaris' hand. "We are honored. It has been a long time since I welcomed a Dutch police officer. Did you have a good flight?"

The commissaris smiled and mumbled a polite phrase. They were standing at the bar of the airport.

"Jenever?" Silva asked. "Or rum? Rum is the drink here."

"Do you make rum in Curaçao?"

"Two daiquiris," Silva said to the barman. "No," he said, "we don't make anything here. The rum comes from Jamaica, packed in drums, rum jelly. We mix it with water in a little factory somewhere. Your health!"

They drank and the commissaris smacked his lips. The iced rum cocktail went down well. The twinge in his legs had gone again. He wondered if he should tell Silva about it; he suddenly felt very friendly.

"Silva," he said, "that's a Portuguese name, isn't it?"

Silva nodded. "Yes. There are many Portuguese names on the island, and Spanish, and English. But I am Dutch. I was born here but I studied in Holland and I came back. Most of us don't come back."

"You like your island," the commissaris said.

"Yes. I love the island. It's nothing but a dry rock, of course."

The commissaris sipped his rum and studied the tall

healthy-looking man, trying vainly to place him, but none of the general information his brain stored would fit. It seemed as if he belonged to a different species of man, in spite of the blue eyes and the dark brown hair. He had seen healthy suntanned men with blue eyes and dark brown hair before. A policeman, definitely. That much was clear. He would have recognized him as a policeman anywhere but when he tried to find out what, in particular, made Silva a policeman, he was groping again. Well, he would find out later.

"A dry rock?" he asked. "But you have beaches, surely, and the sea is all around."

"The sea is there," Silva said. "It's always there, nibbling at our foundation. The rock is mushroom-shaped, standing on a slim stem and the sea keeps on eating it away. One day the stem will break and we will all go down. But the rock itself is bare. It supports some hotels, and the refineries, and the tourists and the oilmen spend their money here and meanwhile we sit around and drink a little, and gamble a little, and gossip about each other and tomorrow is another day."

The commissaris laughed. "That sounds all right."

Silva's face lit up and he touched the commissaris lightly on the forearm. "I thought you Dutchmen didn't like idlers."

"We do, if we are honest enough to admit it. But you are Dutch yourself, you say."

"Island Dutch; it's a different brand."

A constable brought the commissaris' suitcase and the commissaris stared at the blue uniform. Silva noticed the stare.

"You recognize the uniform?"

"It's identical," the commissaris said, amazed, "exactly the same. Our uniform. I thought you would wear khaki and shorts and leather straps."

"I have one like it at home," Silva said.

"So have I," the commissaris said, still amazed.

But the landscape they were seeing from the car had nothing to do with the green pastures of Holland. The low barren hills hid the horizon; some tiny little black boys tended a small herd of goats. "We call them cabryts," Silva said. "Their milk tastes good and the cheese is even better, if you can acquire the taste. Cow's milk is expensive, a macamba's drink."

"Macamba?"

"A Macamba is a Dutchman, a Holland-born Dutchman who doesn't speak the local language, Papiamiento, a mixture of many languages."

"I am a macamba," the commissaris said. "I didn't know."

The constable laughed. "Macamba is a bad word, sir," he said.

"An insult?"

"Yes," Silva said. "The true Dutch aren't very popular. They make all the money."

"But you are accepted?"

"I am from the island," Silva said, "born and bred. I was brought up with cabryt milk and rum, I speak the language. I understand the poor people of the island. If I didn't I would never solve a single crime."

"Do they keep you busy?"

"No, not really. The island is small, one hundred and forty thousand people on three hundred square miles, everybody knows everything. Some fighting and thieving and that's it, but the island is dangerous. There's always a chance of explosion. Too much poverty, too little security and a mixture of races. Once the island was the center of the slave trade. Nobody has forgotten."

"I see," the commissaris said. He was wondering what the island would have been like when the first Spanish vessel sighted its coast. According to his books it would have been covered with trees. "It's us," the commissaris thought. "We are the curse of the planet; the earth would still be beautiful if there had never been any people."

* * *

They were in town now, entering Willemstad from the
north. The town looked neat, with villas and gardens.
Some of the houses were seventeenth-century Dutch in
style but the colors differed. The commissaris had never
seen a pink, or a yellow, or a palish-green gable house
before. "Lovely town," he said, and obviously meant the
compliment and Silva smiled and touched the commissaris' forearm again. "Good thing de Gier isn't here," the
commissaris thought. "Just the sort of thing he would
immediately try to imitate," but he didn't mind. He still
felt friendly.

"I am taking you to a hotel close to my office, in Punda,
on the other side of the harbor. You can have a bath and
rest a little, and have a meal perhaps, and I'll meet you
later this evening or tomorrow morning, if you like."

The commissaris closed the door behind the fat smiling
black man who had taken his suitcase up and brought a tray
with a large glass of orange juice and a pot of coffee. He
had the world to himself now, until the next morning,
when he would see Silva at the police station. There was
no need to do anything about the case tonight. He was
planning to stay several days anyway, on this mysterious
island which would have to be the culmination of all his
imaginary travels through books. He was, he thought—as
he looked out of the window at the lamplit quay where,
through the passing cars, he could see the silhouettes of
schooners moored in an orderly row—very far from his
ordinary routine. He had, wondering whether the thought
was too far-fetched, died and he was born again. This
island, this naked rock as Silva had said, this rock sur-
rounded by a tropical sea could in no way be compared to
the moist fertile bog covered and protected by low gray
clouds which had frustrated, but also sheltered, his mind
for more than sixty years. He felt, as he drank his orange
juice, close to the origin of all that had mystified his wish
to know, close to the terrible secret. He smiled, and

rubbed his legs, which still didn't hurt. Terrible, no doubt. The secret of life, which he had never solved, and probably never would solve, would have to be terrible. But he didn't feel frightened.

The hum of the powerful air conditioner controlling the room's temperature began to irritate him and he switched it off and opened the windows. There weren't as many cars on the quay now, and he could hear the voices of the men on the schooners. High voices, speaking Spanish. The voices were quarreling. "La vaina! No joda, hombre! Santa Purísima!" Swear words no doubt, but he liked the sound. The last two words, shouted by a high-pitched breaking voice, would mean "pure saint." A man, befuddled by rum and the fatigue that comes from a day spent on a tough sea, calling the mother. The mother of all of us, the commissaris agreed, my mother as well, mother of the swamp, mother of the rock. Holy mother, who cares for the sailor and for me, an old weasel sworn to catch the murdering rabbit. For the murderer would be caught, there was no doubt in his mind. Maria van Buren, the fashionable whore in Amsterdam, the dead woman whose death was to be revenged. Order had been disturbed, order would be restored. We cannot allow a man to throw a knife into the living back of a fellow-citizen. He sighed, and stirred his coffee, mechanically patting his pocket to find his tin of cigars. Did he really care? Perhaps he did, perhaps part of his mind cared.

The voices petered out and he heard the sound of little waves which died against the timber of the schooners. The sea lapping gently, eating the island's foundation. At home the sea was lapping at the dikes, waiting patiently for the day that it could flood the swamp and squeeze the life out of its inhabitants, creating new living space for its own denizens, for the sharks, and the turtles, and the dolphins and the myriads of little creatures who would become the new citizens of Amsterdam, covering its streets and buildings and bridges with their shells and waving leaves and creepers and flitting in and out through broken windows.

He closed the windows again, switched on the air conditioner, and ran his bath. A little later he was comfortably soaking, sucking contentedly on his cigar. And when the bath ceremony was over and he had stubbed out the cigar he slipped between the sheets and switched off the light and sighed, and before the sigh had come to its end he had sunk away into nothing, dropping through a hole in his consciousness, and stopped existing.

He seemed to wake up in the same moment, but it was eight hours later and he shaved and dressed and walked down the stairs in a new shantung suit which his wife had bought with him and which was meant for their next holiday in France, a holiday which they had postponed many times because of his faltering health.

He breakfasted by himself, a huge meal consisting of fried eggs and tomatoes and sausages and bacon, and looked at his watch. He had several hours to himself before Silva would be expecting him in the police station. In the hotel's courtyard the fat happy room-waiter was playing with a small dog, talking to the animal in Papiamiento. The walls of the courtyard were covered with creeping plants, carrying a heavy load of many-colored flowers, of which he recognized the bougainvillaea contrasting its subtle violet petals with the loud yellows and reds and sparkling blues of its mates. He crossed the quay and saw the schooners and stopped to look at their loads of vegetables, attractively displayed under awnings of striped sailcloth. An Indian shouted at him, recommending the quality of his cabbages.

"No, thank you," the commissaris said in English. "I live in the hotel you see. Where do you come from?"

The Indian pointed at the sea. "Colombia."

"I see," the commissaris said, and nodded at the man who returned his smile. "You have a beautiful boat."

"Wait," the Indian said suddenly, and ran into the

cabin of his boat. He came back with a pack of cigarettes which he gave to the commissaris.

"Cigarettes from my country. Very good. Black tobacco with sugar. You like."

The commissaris took the packet and turned it around in his hands. It showed the crudely drawn head of a red Indian and he read the brand name "Pielroja."

"How much?"

"No. Present. For you."

The commissaris pocketed the cigarettes, shook the Indian's hand, and walked away slowly. Santa Purísima, the commissaris was thinking, holy mother. Two of your children have met. He crossed the bridge connecting the two parts of Willemstad and, to his right, saw the harbor where white cruise ships and the refineries' tankers and dirty tramp steamers were moored, as safely as on an inland lake. At the other side he looked at shop windows. It was early, not yet nine o'clock, but the Jewish store owners had opened up already and were waiting for their customers, sweating behind the counters with moist armpits or hovering in the street, close to their doors. He studied a display of canned foods. Everything seemed to come from the United States.

"Morning," the merchant said. "What can I do for you today? I have some nice strawberries, in their own juice, and cans of Dutch cream. Your wife will be pleased if you take them home."

"My wife is in Holland," the commissaris said. "I am only here for a few days."

"Holland," the merchant said, "in Holland you can have fresh strawberries. I suggested the wrong thing. What size does your wife wear? I have some batik dresses from Singapore."

The commissaris bought a batik dress. It was expensive and the merchant took ten percent off although the commissaris hadn't said anything.

"Where are you from?" he asked the merchant.

"From Poland. I arrived during the war."

"Before the war," the commissaris said. "You mean before the war."

"No," the merchant said, "during the war. In 1941. I came on a ship which had to sail around for a very long time because nobody wanted us. We were all Jews. Curaçao took us in the end. We had no more fuel and no more money and there was nowhere left to go."

The commissaris shook his head. "You are happy here?"

The merchant took his time parceling up the dress. "Yes. I am happy. I am alive. I earn a living."

"And you?" the merchant asked. "What do you do?"

"I work for the government," the commissaris said.

"Good," the merchant said. "It's always good to work for the government. And Holland has a good government, I hear. That's doubly good. You are lucky."

"Yes," the commissaris said, and put the parcel under his arm. "Thank you. Have a good day."

"Shalom," the merchant said.

"Shalom means 'peace,' doesn't it?" the commissaris asked.

"Peace," the merchant said, "peace on your way."

"Holy Mother," the commissaris said to himself, "don't overdo it. If I meet any more of your children today I will cry."

He passed a church and went in. A black priest was doing something at the altar. A sugary statue of Maria dominated the small ornate space, her plaster-of-Paris dress, pink and light blue and purple, set off a silly inane face.

"That's the way we see you, Holy Mother," the commissaris said, and left the church but he had spent a full five minutes in contemplation and the priest had turned around and seen the old man in the shantung suit with the brown paper parcel under his arm staring at the statue and had crossed himself because he had recognized a faith which he, himself, had often felt and he was a good priest although he had been drunk the night before and lost part of his small wage in a poker game.

A fat woman accosted the commissaris in the street.

"Numbers?" she asked, waving a little book at him.

"No, thank you, madam," the commissaris said.

"You don't play the numbers?" the woman asked. "Macamba, you will have no luck. The numbers are good today, you will win money and you can go to Campo and find yourself a beautiful woman like me."

"Campo?" the commissaris asked.

The woman laughed a loud belly laugh. "You don't know Campo Alegre, the camp of the putas, Curaçao's heaven? How long have you been here?"

"I arrived yesterday."

"You still have time," the fat woman said.

He gave her two guilders and they thought of a number together and she scribbled it in her book with a pencil stub. He lifted his hat and she squeezed his forearm. The fat woman's hand was strong and he was rubbing his arm. "They all do it," he thought. "I'll be black and blue soon."

He wandered back, slowly, holding on to his brown parcel and stopping for coffee and orange juice. He smoked a cigar sitting on a cane chair on the sidewalk, rubbing his legs which didn't hurt, wondering what his wife would say if he told her that they would go and live here, and eventually he found himself back at the hotel where he stripped and took a shower and dressed again.

"Morning," Silva said, touching his forearm with gentle fingers and patting him softly on the shoulder. "Did you sleep well? This is the first time you have been in the tropics I believe."

"Yes," the commissaris said. "I slept very well. I even went for a walk this morning."

"It must be very interesting to see the island for the first time. What did you do?"

The commissaris described some of his adventures and Silva listened, smiling and urging him on.

"You did very well," Silva said, "and the Indian gave you a pack of cigarettes. Amazing. They only come here to cheat us with their vegetables, asking outrageous prices because we can't buy them anywhere else anyway and then they sail home again, laughing at us. But one of them gave you a present. Let me see the pack, please."

The commissaris gave him the cigarettes and Silva held them on the palm of his hand.

"Pielroja," he said, "excellent cigarettes. I have often told the merchants to stock them but they prefer the American brands which all taste the same."

"Keep it. I only smoke cigars."

"No," Silva said, returning the pack, "you must take it home to show it to your friends. I sometimes go to Colombia and I buy them over there. But it's very kind of you all the same. Thank you.

"Now," Silva said, "you want to know about Maria van Buren, who was once called Maria de Sousa and who is now dead."

"Yes."

"I am glad you came," Silva said, "it's hard to talk to somebody on the telephone, especially if you don't know who you are talking to. This island of ours is a maze and how can I explain a maze talking into a piece of plastic?"

"It's difficult," the commissaris agreed.

"But you are here now and I can see your face. So now it's easier."

"Please tell me about her," the commissaris said.

11

"YES," Chief Inspector Silva said, "I will tell you what I know. Some of it I have only found out very recently and some of it I have known for some time but even if you add it all up it may come to nothing."

The commissaris shivered, and Silva immediately showed concern.

"You haven't caught a chill, have you? It's this damned air conditioning. It's a comfort of course but a danger at the same time. This isn't our best season and the heat hits you like a hot towel when you step outside but here, in the office, it's too cool. I'll turn the machine down a little."

"No, no," the commissaris said quickly, "I feel quite well, better, in fact, than I have felt in a long time. But I did, probably, shiver because of the change of temperature."

"All right. Maria de Sousa. But it's intricate, how can I begin to tell you about what goes on here, on the isla. Isla, we call it, a Spanish word. So many influences are acting and reacting together here that the climate, the mental climate, has a very strange character of itself. A peculiar character.''

He paused and the commissaris waited.

''To begin with, everybody knows about everybody. I even know Maria personally, but if nobody had ever introduced us, if we had never gone to the same parties, or met on the beach, even then I would know her by name. And she would know about me. If you had mentioned my name in Amsterdam she could have told you a long story about me, possibly with a lot of truth in it although some of the details would have been grossly exaggerated. We *do* exaggerate here.''

''Yes,'' the commissaris said.

''She comes from a good family. Her father is in business, legitimate business. He owns a wholesale company. He is also engaged in smuggling, but smuggling isn't illegal here, as long as no weapons are involved, or drugs. The Colombians bring us a lot of coffee, no duty is paid, and the bags are marked 'Curaçao produce.' We grow no coffee here, of course. Nothing grows here except thorn trees and cactus and maybe some figs on the old plantations where the soil hasn't been tilled for many years. The Curaçao coffee is sold at very competitive prices but the merchants make a profit for they can undercut the official export trade from the South American continent, and the smugglers who bring us the coffee also make a profit for they pay no tax and the price we pay them is higher than their own governments will pay. But our merchants are very clever. They don't pay in money but in goods, in whisky and cigarettes which the smugglers take back when they return.''

''A profit is made both ways,'' the commissaris said, ''and no local laws are broken.''

''Exactly. Some of the merchants grow very rich.''

''Does old Mr. de Sousa have many children?''

Silva smiled. ''He has three daughters by his wife.''

''There are other children?''

"Yes," Silva said. "There are others. A rich merchant will have mistresses. Some of them will live in adobe huts in the cunucu and others will live in Miami, in expensive apartments."

"Please continue," the commissaris said. "I am sorry I interrupted."

"Mr. de Sousa's daughters are beautiful and it was easy for them to find husbands, husbands the old man would approve of. Maria was the last to marry and she married an engineer, a proper Dutchman who, for a year or so, tried to start a small factory here but he gave up in the end. He had labor problems, our people are not very efficient perhaps, and textiles can be imported here from any country in the world. The shareholders of the company he worked for told him to give up. Mr. de Sousa wasn't pleased with the failure but there was nothing he could do about it, and Maria and her husband went to Holland. Then she divorced him, and she didn't marry again. Some rumors filtered back to us. It seemed she lived an immoral life, but she was living it at a great distance and we weren't concerned. She used to come twice a year and her father would meet her at the airport and take her home. Her father *was* concerned. He would hardly speak to her. After a while he stopped meeting her at the airport. There was a fight, he called her 'puta,' whore, and she was no longer allowed to live in his house, but she still kept coming, living in the same hotel where you live now."

The commissaris shivered again and Silva jumped from his chair. "Just a minute," he said, "I'll get you some very hot tea laced with rum and with a few drops of lemon juice." He was gone for a few minutes while the commissaris enjoyed the view of the harbor. A dirty-looking tramp flying the Venezuelan flag was moored practically underneath the window, separated from the police station by the quay only. An old man with a yellow beard and a torn cap stood on the bridge and looked up. When he saw the commissaris he shouted something and shook his fist, then he disappeared into the cabin and a thick cloud of sooty smoke bulged from the ship's ancient funnel, spreading out slowly and blocking the view from the office.

"Here is your tea," Silva said.

"Somebody was shaking his fist at me," the commissaris said, "an old man with a yellow beard."

Silva laughed and looked out of the window.

"The old bastard has done it again. He probably thought it was I at the window. I caught him once, he was making a nuisance of himself in an expensive bar, and we arrested him. He broke a bottle on a sergeant's skull so he got locked up for a while. Ever since he tries to moor in that convenient spot over there so that he can smoke us out but we have air conditioning and he doesn't worry us. He is a nice old chap when he isn't drunk."

"You don't mind this soot?"

"No," Silva said. "I keep him happy. Sometimes I run out to his ship and shake *my* fist at *him*."

The commissaris sipped his tea and tittered.

"Did you like that story?" Silva asked.

"Yes. Very much."

"Good. So Maria kept coming back to the island in spite of the fact that she was no longer welcome in the house of her parents. I could understand her father's attitude. The women who leave the island become free and they are a bad example, we think, to the women who stay. Here a woman is either very respectable or a whore. The mother is venerated and the father does as he pleases. Maria had opened herself to criticism when she divorced her husband. And she didn't remarry which made it worse. She was a beautiful woman, and educated, so why wouldn't she remarry?"

"Yes," the commissaris said.

"I thought she had a lover here but it seems she hadn't. I made investigations at the hotel and she never shared her room when she was here. They wouldn't have allowed it, I imagine. It isn't that sort of a hotel; important guests stay there, like yourself.''

"Thank you," the commissaris said.

Silva grinned. "Did you like your tea?''

"Very much.''

"Another?''

"Please.''

While Silva was away the commissaris looked out of the window again and saw the captain with the flamboyant beard pacing on his bridge. He waved. The captain ran into his cabin and the commissaris expected another cloud of soot but the captain returned with a pair of binoculars. The two large glass eyes stared and the commissaris waited. The captain put his binoculars down and unsteadily moved his hand, which, when Silva had returned and had joined the commissaris at the window, immediately became a fist again.

"Let's leave him for a while," Silva said. "He may have a heart attack or delirium. Last year he ran into the station downstairs shouting that all the crabs of the island were after him, turning their eyes on stalks and snapping at his legs with their wicked shears.''

"Poor fellow," the commissaris said, and sat down.

"Oh, he is all right. He is quite old and he has had a good life on the Carribbean. He won't admit he is old, that's why he dyes his beard. I like him, I'll be sorry when he goes. Maria used to know him too. I have seen them talking together. He has probably offered her a free trip but I don't think she has ever put a foot on his boat. His crew are a bunch of madmen.''

"So Maria didn't have a lover," the commissaris said.

"Not here. When I knew you were coming out I alerted my detectives and they must have alerted their contacts on the island. The information I was given tallies. Two reasons brought Maria back to the island. Plain homesickness and her contact with Shon Wancho.''

"Ah," the commissaris said.

"Not what you think. Shon Wancho is old, seventy years old maybe, and he is a black man. Maria isn't altogether white herself, most people aren't over here. I am not white either."

"You?" the commissaris asked.

"I look white, I know, but my hair is a bit kinky. My sister is much darker than I am. It all depends on the laws of Mendel and the way the chromosomes go. Maria is darker than her sisters. Shon Wancho is pitch black. He is an important man, a local character who is feared and respected. That's why he isn't called Wancho but *Shon* Wancho, a title of respect, like Don in Spanish."

"He is a sorcerer," the commissaris said.

Silva brought his hand down on the desk with some force. "You know?"

The commissaris didn't answer but brought out an object packed in tissue paper. He carefully unfolded the paper and put the contents on Silva's desk. "Do you know what these are?"

Silva put on a pair of spectacles. He studied the mandrake roots. "No, I have never seen them before. They are roots, I can see that, and they look evil. Amazing, isn't it, they look like thin men, human beings. That little twig is very much like a penis and the legs are perfectly formed and they have heads and arms. And those hairy bodies, there is even hair on the heads and those dark spots are eyes."

He crossed himself.

"Yes," the commissaris said. "They scare me too. We found them in Maria van Buren's houseboat. We found plants as well, herbs, witch-weeds. She grew them in pots on her windowsills. The roots are of the mandrake plant, they were said to be powerful."

"So you suspected her of sorcery?"

"It isn't a crime," the commissaris said, "so we couldn't suspect her of it. Black magic is still practiced and we have run into it before. Dolls with pins in them, people collecting other people's nail clippings and hairs. It may be more popular over here but perhaps it will become fashionable in Europe again. The hippies are fascinated by it and the drug cult, it seems, is related to black magic."

"And these are mandrake roots? I have never heard of mandrake."

The commissaris told Silva what he knew about the plant and Silva listened.

"Gruesome. And you are right about Shon Wancho being a sorcerer. He lives by himself in an adobe hut at the extreme north of the island, near Westpoint. He hardly ever leaves his place but people will go and see him."

"Do you know him?" the commissaris said.

"Yes. Not well, but I have met him. We had a killing out there once and I went to his hut to ask if he had seen anything. It turned out that he knew nothing about the case. It had been a drunken fight and the killer gave himself up the next day."

"And what did you think of Mr. Wancho?"

Silva rubbed his face. "I liked him. Yes, I really liked him. He has a beautiful face, very quiet and peaceful. I was, to tell you the truth, immensely impressed by him and I have often thought of him since."

"You don't think he was an evil man?"

"No. Not at all. He struck me as a man who knows himself, and therefore knows others. Socrates said that, I believe. The greatest feat is to know yourself. I think Shon Wancho is a wise man."

"And Maria went to see him?"

"She did, according to my contacts. Every time she visited the island she would hire a car and go out there each day. She would leave the hotel after breakfast and come back before nightfall. But I don't know what she did out there. Nobody but Shon Wancho himself would know. His place is close to the sea and hidden behind some cliffs and I don't think anyone would dare to spy on the old man."

"Hmm," the commissaris said, "I will have to go out there."

"Perhaps you should."

"And I will have to go and see her father. He knows about her death, I assume."

"We informed him," Silva said.

"He knows she was murdered?"

"He does. He was very upset although he tried not to show it."

"I'll have to hire a car."

"No," Silva said. "I will give you a police car and a driver."

"I would rather have a map of the island. I'll see more if I have to find my own way."

"As you like," Silva said. "I'll go down to the garage with you and we will give you an unmarked car."

12

GRIJPSTRA had been amused when he saw de Gier at the central station of Amsterdam, huddled in a heavy, dark blue duffelcoat and adorned with a binocular case dangling from a leather strap, but now he envied the sergeant, who stood at the railing of the ferry, warm and comfortable under his load of cloth while Grijpstra felt the wind go right through his thin raincoat and had to hang on to his hat.

"Beautiful," said de Gier, who had been looking down at the sea. The waves were short and choppy and gray, reflecting the heavy clouds above them.

"What?" Grijpstra asked.

"The sea," de Gier said, "and the sky, and the island over there."

Schiermonnikoog was showing itself as a dark green line on the horizon. The overgrown dikes, a man-made barrier to protect the rich grazing land of the south of the island, interrupted the wide fluid space of the shallow Waddensea all around them. Seagulls were floating above and just behind the ship, effortless, keeping themselves in balance with slight flicks of the ends of their wings.

"It's cold," Grijpstra said. "Spring is warmer in the city."

"But we are not in the city, we are here. Look at the birds. We'll see a lot of birds on the island, it's a bird's paradise."

"I know," Grijpstra said. "I have been here before. But it was warmer then, toward the end of July. I camped with the kids."

His voice sounded gruff. De Gier stopped looking at the sea. "You didn't like it?"

"The kids enjoyed it."

"Did *you* like it?"

"No."

"Why not?"

"Too full. There were so many tents and beach cabins and people pulling carts and pushing bicycles that I thought the damn island would sink. Everything was full, you had to wait half an hour before they would serve you in the restaurants. And sand, sand everywhere. There was a gale blowing most of the time and we nearly lost the tent. The lines broke and it tried to fly into the sea. The sand got into my nose, I had to pick it all the time."

"It'll be all right now, the holidays haven't started yet."

Grijpstra eyed the approaching strip of land suspiciously. It had begun to rain.

"You don't look like a birdwatcher," de Gier said. "You look like a policeman. Don't you have a cap in your suitcase? Nobody wears a hat here."

"No," Grijpstra said guiltily, "but I'll put my hat in my bag, it keeps blowing away anyway. And maybe they'll have a coat like yours in the shops."

"I thought my duffelcoat was silly, you made a lot of funny remarks about it on the train."

"It looks silly, but I had forgotten we were going to be birdwatchers."

"Never mind," de Gier said pleasantly. "Do you know anything about birds?"

"Seagulls."

"That's something. Any other birds?"

"Swans."

"There won't be any here."

"Sparrows," Grijpstra said impatiently. "What does it matter? If there are any experts out there they'll be airing their knowledge and all I have to do is say they are right. Do you know anything about birds?"

"Sure," de Gier said. "I even have a book on birds. I studied it last night. Oystercatchers with red beaks, and coot, two types of coot, with a white spot on the head and with a red spot on the head, and mallards and . . . ."

"Yes," Grijpstra said in a loud voice.

"What yes?"

"I know. Don't try to impress me. I know what a mallard is. A mallard is a plain silly fat Amsterdam duck sitting on the canal. Every day I see a hundred mallard, two hundred mallard, three hundred . . ."

His voice was rising.

"All right," de Gier said. "You know what a mallard is. But do you know what a cormorant is?"

"I don't care," Grijpstra said, and sneezed.

"You still have your cold."

"The cold is O.K."

De Gier studied his friend's face. Grijpstra didn't look well. The skin of his face seemed to have lost its elasticity and his eyes had sunk a little into their sockets.

"Wait," de Gier said, and went into the passengers' cabin. He bought two paper cups filled with hot creamy coffee and four fat sausages, packed in thick plastic skins.

"Have some coffee," he said, and passed the cup carefully to Grijpstra. "Mind, it's hot. You haven't had breakfast, we should have eaten something on the train."

Grijpstra stared at the coffee swirling in the paper cup. Little bubbles had formed on the surface and the bubbles turned in irregular circles.

De Gier gulped his coffee, and took a sausage out of his pocket. "Good sausages," he said. "I have two for you as well, but finish your coffee first."

He began to peel the plastic skin off the little roll of solid fat meat.

Grijpstra looked at the sausage, threw his cup overboard, and bent down over the railing. His hat was caught by the wind again but this time he didn't try to grab it.

De Gier looked sadly at his sausage. He opened his hand and it fell into the sea. It sank. He saw Grijpstra's hat, rapidly being tossed about by strong white-headed waves.

"There's your hat," de Gier said, "and you have vomited on my sausage."

Grijpstra vomited again and de Gier walked over to the other side of the ship, where he ate the other three sausages. The ship was now approaching the small harbor of Schiermonnikoog and he collected Grijpstra's and his own suitcase. They met again on the gangway.

"You're all right now?"

Grijpstra nodded, and put his right foot on the island's solid ground.

"You've made it," de Gier said.

Grijpstra turned around, slowly pulling back his heavy right arm. His large hand had become a fist and he was staring at de Gier's chin.

"I am sorry," de Gier said. "I didn't buy those sausages to make you sick. I really thought you might be hungry."

"I wasn't sick, I just felt a little off."

"He wasn't sick," de Gier said to a man walking next to him. "He only vomited a little."

"Happens to the best of us," the man said, "but there will always be people who make fun of others. The minute they see that somebody is in trouble they laugh. There are some pretty nasty people about nowadays.''

"You've got a friend," de Gier said to Grijpstra.

They didn't speak to each other again until the bus which had picked them up dropped them in the center of the little town and the driver had directed them to a hotel.

They took a double room and Grijpstra immediately opened his suitcase and began to rummage about it. He put on a pair of thick corduroy trousers and a heavy workman's jersey. His feet went into a pair of old boots, and a muffler appeared which he wound around his neck.

"Now," he said.

"That's better. But you need a coat."

"You go out and buy me something."

"I may buy the wrong thing."

"No," Grijpstra said. "You are supposed to be a man of taste. You know my size. I'll go down and play billiards and phone the adjutant of the state police. He'll come and join me and we can have a talk and make some plans. This afternoon we can begin to sniff about the island. I want to see IJsbrand Drachtsma's house and speak to some people who know him. Later we can come out in the open. Perhaps it'll shake him when he knows that we are making investigations."

"Right," de Gier said, and went out. He found three shops where clothes were sold but there weren't any duffelcoats. Finally he bought a yellow oilcloth jacket and a pair of huge trousers to go with it and a souwester, all of the same material. The shopkeeper promised that he would swap them for something else if the client wasn't satisfied. He found Grijpstra in the barroom of the hotel, a low-ceilinged smoky place where he was playing billiards with a square-looking small man in a blue suit with shiny elbows and a white shirt and a tie.

"Adjutant Buisman," the square-looking man said.

"Pleased to meet you, sergeant. I heard some stories about you when Grijpstra spent his holiday here."

"What sort of stories?"

"Good stories," Grijpstra said. "You can join us if you promise not to tear the felt, and you have to chalk the cue before you play."

"All right," de Gier said, "is it my turn now?"

"Go ahead."

De Gier studied the position of the two white balls and the single red one.

"Which ball?"

"The one closest to you."

It was an easy shot and the two adjutants waited for de Gier to spoil it. De Gier chalked the cue and studied the balls again.

"Go on," Buisman said.

De Gier flicked the cue and his ball shot away, hitting the red ball on the side and the white ball full on. It was a rude shot but he had made a point.

Buisman looked at Grijpstra.

"Good," Grijpstra said, "but you won't make the next one."

The balls were well apart now and de Gier began to chalk his cue again. He would have to work out the right angle and use the table's elastic sides. He tried to remember what he had learned at the police school where one of his friends had always insisted that he should play, refusing to buy him a beer if he didn't, and de Gier had been forced to play more often than he wanted to, for his friend had a good allowance from home.

He played and made another point. Buisman showed his approval by stamping his cue on the floor, and ordering three glasses of old cold jenever. De Gier made a third point and a fourth, and Grijpstra began to sweat but then he missed.

"Not bad," Grijpstra said. "I thought you hated all sports except judo?"

"Ach," de Gier mumbled modestly, "it's all a matter of concentration, isn't it?" but he shouldn't have said it. He managed only the easy shots after that and Grijpstra patted him on the shoulder. "Beginner's luck, matey."

Adjutant Buisman shook his head. "I don't know," he said. "The sergeant played well, he needs more practice that's all. How long will you be staying?"

"Not long," Grijpstra said, and he explained the purpose of their visit.

"IJsbrand Drachtsma," the adjutant said softly, "well, I never. I know him well, you know. I have been out on his yacht and he comes here to play billiards sometimes and he has been on the police launch with us. He is a big man on the island, he could be the mayor if he wanted to but he's got other things to do, and you think he is involved with your dead lady?"

"She was his mistress," de Gier said.

"Yes, yes," the adjutant said, "he would chase the ladies in Amsterdam, of course; it's another world out there. Here he goes for walks on the beach and sits near the fire with his wife. She knits. I have a scarf she knit. A beautiful fireplace, I have often been to the house."

He was silent for a while. "But he has an alibi you say?"

"Yes," Grijpstra said.

"So what are you bothering about then?"

Grijpstra told him.

The adjutant was shaking his head. "No evidence at all. Not a shred of it, but you have your suspicions. Christ almighty, you really think he would have paid somebody to kill a nice-looking woman?"

"He may have."

"Sure, he may have and he may not have. You are detectives, maybe you know. I don't, we have never had a killing on the island, not even with the tourists around and there are more of them every year. Running over the island like rats over a body—if we don't stop them one day they'll take all the sand home in their shoes—but we haven't had a crime. They mill about, like lunatics. When the moon is full they are worse than ever. We organize games for them, and walks and competitions. We have to keep them busy you know.''

De Gier was grinning.

''Yes, you laugh, but this used to be a lovely quiet island, beautiful with the birds and seals. We still have them but it has taken a lot of protection, fences and signs, and we have to patrol the reserves. People don't mean any harm and they are obedient enough if you tell them in a nice way but if you aren't watching them every minute of the day they'll stamp on the last egg and tear out the last flower and then they'll look about and wonder why the place is bare.''

''Yes,'' de Gier said, ''I know. We have them milling about Amsterdam every summer.''

''They can't pull the buildings apart. Haven't you got any other suspects, without an alibi?''

''We have,'' Grijpstra said, and he explained the situation but the adjutant kept shaking his head.

''I see what you mean,'' he said in the end. ''He is a strong person, our IJsbrand, and he would be ruthless if somebody went against him. He was a hero during the war I am told, rowed all the way to England and fought his way back, and he is probably as tough as nails in business, but here he is different, very gentle and relaxed. His father was born on the island and I think he considers Schiermonnikoog his real home. He is here most weekends and he doesn't go abroad like other people. When the place gets too full he gets on his yacht, and he has a big garden with a stone wall around it.''

''We are not too sure of his alibi,'' de Gier said. ''We have only the word of two German businessmen, and the commissaris spoke to them on the phone.''

''The war is over,'' the adjutant said.

''Sure.''

"You can trust the Germans nowadays."

"Sure."

"When did you say the lady was murdered?"

"Saturday a week ago."

"It's Sunday now," the adjutant said. "IJsbrand will be in his villa. He was here last weekend, I remember, I saw him in town in the afternoon, after the ferry left, the last ferry. He couldn't have gone to Amsterdam that evening. There's no way to get off the island, no airport, nothing."

"His yacht?" Grijpstra asked. "Surely the yacht is fast, it could get to the coast as quick as the ferry, and it only takes two hours in a fast car to Amsterdam. He has a fast car, a Citroën. He could have been back in his villa the same evening."

"Yes," the adjutant said, "but I think the yacht was here. I'll have to ask my colleague, he was out in the launch that evening. It was a nice night I remember, he often goes out, just for the fun of it. But Drachtsma could have used another boat, of course. There are a lot of boats in the harbor and anybody would lend him a boat if he asked for it."

"Maybe he didn't ask," de Gier said. "If he knew the boats he could have used one and the owner would never know."

Adjutant Buisman thought for a while. "He could have. But these German chaps say they spent the evening at his house and he was with them. Your commissaris will have their names and addresses and he has probably asked the German police to check. Contacts with the foreign police are good nowadays, they tell me."

"Yes," Grijpstra said.

Buisman ordered another round and they drank for a while and smacked their lips and looked at each other.

"Suppose he did send a man to do the job for him, how will you go about proving it? You would have to find the man, wouldn't you?"

"He might be from the island, an old friend from the war days perhaps, somebody who could use a lot of money or somebody who admired him."

"Ah," Buisman said. "The knife. A fighting knife it was, a soldier's knife, and it was thrown. I could find out who knows how to throw a knife. I wouldn't know off-hand. The rangers of the reserves have knives but they wouldn't throw them, and we have knives, we are often on the sea and a knife is always handy in a boat."

" 'We, the police,' you mean?" de Gier asked.

"No." Buisman laughed. "I mean 'we, the people who sail boats.' I have a sailing boat of my own, you know."

"Perhaps you could find out," Grijpstra said. "I admit that we haven't got much to stand on. Perhaps we are only here because we don't know what else to do and the commissaris has gone to Curaçao. He'll be back soon and he'll probably tell us to come back as soon as he sees the note on his desk."

"That's better," the adjutant said. "Let's make a little holiday out of it. I'll see if I can find a knife thrower and you have a bit of a rest and a bit of a walk. You mentioned birdwatching, this is the right time of the year for it. What say if you go to bed early and I pick you up early tomorrow morning. It's mating time now and I can show you some marvelous sights, sights you will never see in the city. How about that?"

Buisman's face was wreathed in smiles and Grijpstra didn't have the heart to refuse, but he tried.

"My friend here is very interested in birds, he was telling me all about it on the ferry. Why don't you go together and I'll see you later tomorrow. I have a bit of a cold." He coughed a few times.

"No," de Gier said quickly. "You come as well. Maybe we'll see some mallards."

"Yes, you come too," Buisman said, getting up. "Mallards you can see anywhere but here I can show you six or seven different types of duck and there are others, really rare birds which I want to show you. See you tomorrow.''

"What time will you be here?'' Grijpstra asked, trying his best to make his voice sound eager.

"Early,'' Buisman said. "It'll have to be early or we won't see anything. I'll be here at three-thirty sharp; I'll wait in the street. Put some warm clothes on. Have you got binoculars?''

De Gier nodded.

"You, Grijpstra?''

"No,'' Grijpstra said, "I haven't got any binoculars.''

"Never mind. I'll borrow a pair from the police station. They are heavy but they are better than mine. You'll have to be careful for they cost a fortune. Well, have a good time.''

"Shit,'' Grijpstra said as the door closed behind the adjutant. "Shit and shit again. Now why did you have to get *me* into it? You got me sick cn the boat with your revolting sausage, peeling the skin off it as if it were a boiled monkey's pecker, and now you want me to stump through the mud in the middle of the night to see a lot of floppy birds jumping at each other. A joke is a joke but this is ridiculous. Sometimes you overdo it, you know.''

He was red in the face and thumping the table with his fist.

"Do you think I like it?'' de Gier said, his face just as red. "And who was telling the adjutant that I liked birds. You know I was only egging you on on the ferry. What do I know about coot and cormorants and whatnots? Just a few names I happened to remember. We need this man, don't we? And we can't upset him by refusing his invitations? I don't like drinking jenever in the middle of the day but I accepted just to please him. And I don't like playing billiards. And I am damned if I'll walk through the mud while you are stinking and snoring in your bed.''

Grijpstra had begun to laugh and de Gier, after having tried unsuccessfully to stare him down, joined him. Soon they were hiccuping and helplessly patting the table.

Grijpstra shouted for more jenever and they finished up playing billiards, giggling at each other.

"Three-thirty in the morning," de Gier said.

"Promise never to tell anyone."

"I promise," de Gier said.

They shook hands and went to the dining room for a late lunch.

By nine o'clock that night they were fast asleep, worn out by thirty games of billiards and some seven or eight glasses of old cold jenever each.

13

"EXCUSE ME," a pleasant well-modulated voice said. "Do you mind if I sit down at your table for a moment?"

The commissaris looked up from his plate of fried noodles and shrimps. He had been eating and looking at the map, spread out on the table next to his plate, at the same time. He felt a little perturbed by the interruption; he had refused Silva's invitation to lunch in order to be by himself and he had, after having walked about for a few minutes, found a cheap clean-looking Chinese restaurant where he could enjoy his favorite food. And now there was someone else, standing patiently next to him and wanting something.

"Please," the commissaris said, "please sit down." He shook hands.

"Van der Linden," the neatly dressed man said. "I saw you at the airport yesterday, I saw you again in the lounge of the hotel last night and now I see you for the third time in two days. In Curaçao it is quite unheard of to meet the same man three times in two days without knowing his name, so I have taken the liberty of making your acquaintance."

The commissaris smiled, looking at the face of the old gentleman. Mr. van der Linden would probably be close to seventy but a pair of very alive eyes twinkled in his face which seemed to be covered with old white-yellowish leather.

"I am a tourist," the commissaris said. "Surely you must see thousands of tourists wandering through your city."

Mr. van der Linden smiled and the waxed ends of his mustache vibrated. "No, sir. Excuse me for contradicting you. You are not a tourist."

"No?" the commissaris asked.

"No. A tourist has no purpose. He wanders about, looking at the shop windows. He wears an open shirt with a flower pattern, or striped, and he talks in a loud voice. He has to, for otherwise he loses his identity."

"Ah."

"A tourist doesn't wear a shantung suit with a waistcoat. Your waistcoat intrigues me. I haven't seen anyone wear a waistcoat for years."

The commissaris looked down at his waistcoat. "It went with the suit," he said guiltily, "and it isn't warm. It isn't lined, you see. And it has handy pockets. I always wear a waistcoat. My lighter goes into the left pocket and my watch into the right. It's a matter of habit."

Mr. van der Linden roared with laughter. "You don't have to explain yourself to me," he said. "It's I who should explain myself. I am a lawyer, you see, I have practiced here for many years, more than I can remember, and I didn't leave when I retired. I got used to the place. You are a police officer, aren't you?"

"Yes," the commissaris said.

"You are here to investigate the death of Maria van Buren."

"Yes."

"I was expecting a Dutch police officer to come out. Usually when one of us gets into trouble out there the causes can be found here."

"Do you have an idea that could help me?" the commissaris asked, opening his tin of cigars and holding it out.

"No, thank you. I am not allowed to smoke anymore. It's a great pity. We always have Cuban cigars here and to smoke one in the evening, sitting under the tamarind tree in the garden, is a true pleasure. *Was* a true pleasure. Yes, perhaps I have an idea. You found what Maria was doing out there, in Amsterdam I mean. It's 'out there' to me now, strange isn't it, and I am a true Dutchman."

"A macamba," the commissaris said.

"You have been learning already. Maria was a very courageous girl. She had ideals, strange ideals. Some girls have ideals, not too many of them, fortunately perhaps. They might stop having children one day and it would be the end of us."

"It might be the best ideal of all," the commissaris said, trying to blow a smoke ring.

"Yes. Quite. An interesting theory. Will you be staying long?"

The commissaris shook his head.

"Pity. I have a bottle of old brandy left and we could drink it under my tree and discuss a world without people. It's a beautiful thought. We wouldn't be there to regret the fact that we wouldn't be there."

"Maria was the mistress of at least three rich men," the commissaris said.

"Yes. My mind was wandering. It often does, nowadays. But Maria wasn't a prostitute. I knew her as a child and I think she had the mind of a discoverer, and explorer. She wanted to find out. She liked men, of course, any beautiful woman does. Men will confirm the fact that a woman is beautiful. I think she was experimenting with manipulating people."

"And somebody objected and killed her."

"That's one possibility," Mr. van der Linden said. "Another thought which occurred to me was that somebody would object to her way of life in general."

"We have reason to believe that she dabbled in sorcery."

"Sorcery," Mr. van der Linden repeated, and laughed.

"You don't believe in sorcery?"

"Of course I believe in it. I have lived a long time, and most of my life I have spent on this island, and on similar islands. Black magic works, I am convinced of it. It's a lot of mumbo jumbo of course but so is advertising, and nobody will deny that advertising works. But black magic is silly, like advertising."

"Magic is silly?" the commissaris asked.

"*Black* magic is. Not the real thing. Black magic is a perversion of the real thing and all perversions are silly. The desire to hurt others is childish."

"You think Maria practiced black magic?"

Mr. van der Linden spread his hands on his knees and looked at them for a while. His body became still, his face relaxed. "Yes," he said in the end.

"Do you think it killed her?"

The commissaris had to wait for the answer again. "Yes," Mr. van der Linden said.

The car bounced a little on a bad patch of tar and the commissaris lost the thread of his thoughts. He had changed the pattern of his theory so that Mr. van der Linden's remarks would fit in, but now he remembered that Silva had told him not to miss the Curaçao forest. The forest was supposed to be two hundred yards long and there would be a dip in the road. If he reached the dip he was supposed to stop the car and get out. Silva had told him to spend at least five minutes in the forest to try to recapture the old atmosphere of the island, the atmosphere that it had in the beginning of the fifteenth century, when Indian tribes still lived in Curaçao, Indians who fished and hunted and who welcomed strangers and took care of them and who built large huts which fitted in with the landscape and whose religion centered around magic.

The car found the dip and the commissaris drove her off the road and switched the engine off and got out. He sat down on a rock and closed his eyes.

"The real thing," he said aloud, "not the perversion." To hurt is the perversion, he thought. So the real thing would be to cure, to restore.

He tried not to think but to feel the trees around him but his mind refused to become calm. He lit a cigar and got back into the car.

He was driving close to the coast and he could hear the sea raging against the cliffs. The forests had given way to the cunucu again, the dried-out veld with thornbushes. An occasional car passed or met him but nothing else moved, except the few cabryt goats tearing at dry plants, and once he had to slow down suddenly for a large lizard which scuffled across the road and gave him an angry look from its heavily lidded eyes.

He had to be close to Shon Wancho's place now and he stopped near a hut. The black woman who had come to the door gave him directions in slow pure Dutch. He thanked her and lifted his hat, and her answering smile was kind and puzzled.

The road didn't go to the house and he had to walk the last half mile until he came to the cliffs.

When he finally found the tall thin black man he felt very hot and his suit stuck to his skin.

"Good afternoon, Shon Wancho," the commissaris said, and took off his hat.

When, later, he tried to remember, to rebuild their meeting he found the task to be impossible. He tried often, he always failed.

There had been, and that seemed to be the main difficulty which made fun with his memory, no real conversation.

Shon Wancho hadn't answered a single question, and after a while the commissaris had stopped asking questions. The experience was weird. As a police officer he had been trained to create situations. The other party, whether suspect or witness, had always been at some considerable disadvantage. He had always managed to trick his opponents, playing on their fear, on their sense of self-importance. And they had talked. Never once had the commissaris failed. He had cornered his opponents, threatened and flattered them. And they had talked. Never once had the commissaris failed. He had cornered his opponents, quietly, by being polite to them, by making a little statement or asking a little question. They had been frightened of going to jail, of losing their reputation. They had been jealous and tried to incriminate others. They cared.

But Shon Wancho didn't care. When the commissaris found him the old man had been working in his garden tending a creeping plant with delicate yellow flowers. The garden was next to a small house, a neat building consisting of two rooms and a covered porch, supported by strong beams which looked as if they had been found on the beach, bleached by a hundred years of sun. Shon Wancho had met his guest, treating the commissaris as if he were a small tired hot child. He had been shown where he could wash his face and hands, had been given some cool fruit juice to drink and directed to a rocking chair in the shadow of the porch from which he could see the flowers of the garden. There had been no need to explain the purpose of his visit. The commissaris had tried but his sentences broke halfway. The quiet half-closed eyes of the thin elegant black man expressed a peaceful lack of interest in the prattling of a distracted mind. He neither answered nor acknowledged the questions of the commissaris but stood silently, leaning against a bleached beam. The commissaris became irritated and began to repeat himself, his words stumbled over each other, he felt as if he were trying to press against something which wasn't there, but at the same time he felt some response in his own mind, as if the tall Negro were right. Nothing had happened so what was the police officer fretting about? He began to pay attention to the silence of his host. He saw Shon Wancho's face now, the small pointed beard, the high cheekbones, the thick arching lips framing the wide mouth, and the aquiline nose, the face of a chief, of a nobleman.

"This man needs nothing," the commissaris' mind was saying to itself and a small surge of approval moved through his thoughts.

"No, not a chief," he was thinking now. "A chief needs a tribe. And a nobleman needs his rank."

His attempts at trying to place the man failed. And suddenly he felt that he no longer cared either. The quietness of Shon Wancho was too strong and he surrendered to it. Shon Wancho had stopped looking at the commissaris. He sat down on a low stool, close to the rocking chair. His back was erect and his gaze steady; he was looking ahead now, at the garden and the distant sea.

Together they underwent the sudden explosive sunset of the tropics; the bursting colors, the wide space of the endless view, and the cool powerful sound of the sea combined to knock away the last support of the busy-ness of the commissaris' mind so that he reached a state of awareness where he was neither awake nor asleep.

After a while he found his hat and put it on and left, and before he left Shon Wancho had lightly touched his forearm and smiled.

"So what did you find out?" the commissaris kept on asking himself as he drove back to Willemstad. "What did you find out?"

There was a final visit to make. He stopped near a public call-box and dialed Mr. de Sousa's number.

Mr. de Sousa answered the phone himself.

"Yes, commissaris," Mr. de Sousa said. "Chief-Inspector da Silva told me you would be calling."

"I would like to come and see you," the commissaris said.

"Tomorrow?"

"No. Tomorrow I should be on my way back to Holland. Unfortunately I am rather pressed for time. If it isn't inconvenient for you I would like to come and see you right now. According to my map I am very close to your house. I should be able to see you within a few minutes."

"You will be welcome," Mr. de Sousa said and rang off.

The commissaris found the house, a palatial home built on a small hill with a driveway lined with palm trees. Mr. de Sousa opened the car door and led the way.

The house breathed wealth. The corridor was wide and high and there were potted plants and pieces of sculpture and oil portraits of men who looked like plantation owners, dressed in riding breeches and holding whips, and of ladies with elaborate hairstyles and stiff lace dresses.

As they walked to Mr. de Sousa's study a servant scuffled behind them carrying a silver tray with bottles and glasses. Polite phrases filled ten minutes before the commissaris could mention the name of Maria.

"Yes," Mr. de Sousa said, and the folds of his face trembled. "My daughter. She is dead."

The commissaris found that it had become impossible to ask questions. He waited.

"I refused her presence," Mr. de Sousa said, and began to wipe his wet face, "my own daughter, the cleverest, the most beautiful of them all. I wouldn't have her in my own house. I disapproved. I had to disapprove. Do you understand, commissaris of police, do you understand?"

The commissaris drank his whisky, the silence of Shon Wancho was still around him and some of it reached the fat rich man and calmed him a little.

"Perhaps you understand. Perhaps you have children of your own. But Europe is different. I have been to Europe, many times. I am a wealthy man, I do big business. I know the beautiful women of Europe, I have paid them money and they have given me experiences which I will never forget. I am grateful to those women. But my own daughter became one of them and that I couldn't accept."

Mr. de Sousa filled the commissaris' glass and fussed with the ice cubes and the water and the silver stirring spoon.

"But I am her father and perhaps I should have accepted. As a child she always came to me and talked to me and we were together. She was a wise child and I learned from her as we walked through the island. I took her to the other islands, the Dutch islands and the English islands and some of the French. I even took her to Haiti, she wanted to go to Haiti. She was partly black and she was very interested in her blackness and Haiti is a black country. I always thought that a father teaches his child but Maria taught *me*. Her voice was very quiet and when she spoke I listened.

"And now she is dead," Mr. de Sousa said after a while. "You will want to know who threw the knife into her but I do not know."

The commissaris returned to his hotel and had a bath. He drank his coffee and his orange juice and he smoked a cigar and the hot water soaked the dirt and the sweat off him. He put on a clean suit and left the hotel and wandered past the ships moored at the quay. The schooner of the Indian who gave him the cigarettes had left. He stopped to admire the old tramp steamer.

"What are you looking at?" a voice bellowed from the bridge.

"Hello," the commissaris shouted.

"You," the captain with the yellow beard shouted back. "You? Come up here!"

The commissaris crossed the gangway, anxious not to

soil his suit. The captain met him on the lower deck.

"Have some rum with me, policeman," the captain said, and put out his hand. The commissaris touched the hand gently but it was clean, clean like its owner, who was now grinning through his beard, showing broken teeth separated by large gaps.

"I saw you at Silva's window this morning," the captain said, and cackled. "He pretends not to care about the soot I blow at him but I got him the other day. He came out and shook his fist at me. That police station will be very dirty when I finish with it but there is nothing they can do about it except cough. I am not breaking any law. I have to keep the old engine going, don't I?"

They were in the captain's cabin, and a hunchback in a torn jacket had brought a flat green bottle of rum and glasses and a dented silver bucket filled with ice.

"Nice bucket," the captain said, picking it up. "Filched it from a nightclub in Barranquilla. But they made me pay for it on the next trip. They always win in the end."

He poured a glass half full of rum and filled it with ice.

"Thank you," the commissaris said.

"Carta Blanca," the captain said, "the best rum of the island. You know why?"

"No."

"Because of the label."

The captain turned the bottle and the commissaris saw a handsome black woman showing a full well-formed bosom as she bent down to look at a letter which she had obviously just received and which was causing a strong emotion.

"Every man who drinks this rum thinks he has written the letter," the captain said, "and they forget the taste of the rum. But the rum isn't bad all the same."

The commissaris leaned back in his chair and sipped a little of the raw-tasting liquor. He told himself to be careful, his body wouldn't take much of the strong spirit.

"You made some money today," the captain said, emptying his glass, filling it again and leering at the commissaris. "I spoke to the woman who sold you a number. You should go to Otrabanda tomorrow and collect, she likes you. You had a busy day, didn't you? One of my men saw you talking to Mr. van der Linden. Did you like the old buzzard?"

"Yes," the commissaris said, "a nice man."

"He is all right. Won a case for me once, and he lost one too, but that was my fault. He warned me but I was young then. I believed in right and wrong."

"You don't anymore?"

"Hee hee." The captain sat down gingerly in a rickety-looking cane chair. "Must be careful now. Chair is getting old, like the ship. One day the bottom will fall out of her but it doesn't matter anymore. We are all getting old, me, the crew, the engine. Right and wrong. I don't know now. The older I get the less I know."

The commissaris forgot his good intentions and swallowed his rum. He put the glass on the table with a bang and the captain filled it up for him. His hand was unsteady and he had trouble with the ice cubes. The commissaris helped him.

"You saw our medicine man today as well, didn't you? Did you like him?"

"Shon Wancho," the commissaris said.

"Shon Wancho," the captain repeated, nodding his head vigorously.

"Do you know him?"

"Sure," the captain said. "I brought him here, a long time ago, thirty years maybe, maybe longer. He comes from the bush, a bush doctor. His father was a bush doctor before him. He knows."

"He knows what?"

The captain gesticulated. "Everything. He knows the lot."

"Do you see him regularly?"

"Not regularly," the captain said, "sometimes. I saw him the other day."

"Why?"

"About the crabs. The crabs were after me, you know. The rum brought them out. Thousands of crabs. I was seeing them all the time, rum or no rum."

"Did he tell you to stop drinking?"

The captain looked surprised. "No," he said, "but he chased the crabs away."

"They haven't come back?"

"If they do I will go and see him again."

The captain was slurring his words and the commissaris expected him to fall asleep or pass out any minute now but he had underestimated the old man's capacity.

"You like Curaçao?" he asked.

The commissaris had suddenly remembered the pain in his legs. The twinge had come back again during the morning but it had left him when he was sitting on the rocking chair in Shon Wancho's house and it wasn't with him now. "This is a good island," he was telling the captain. "I have been thinking that I might like to live here one day."

The captain nodded solemnly. "Yes, you do that. And when you get bored seeing the same people and the same goats you can come on a little trip with me. I have a cabin for passengers and the cook is Chinese."

"That would be nice."

"No charge," the captain said, "provided I am still alive. Don't wait too long."

The captain stamped his foot on the floor twice and an elderly Chinese appeared in the doorway.

"You are Dutch," the captain said, "and the Dutch always eat something when they drink. I have come to Curaçao so often that I have picked up their habits. In Venezuela we drink when we drink. What have you got, cook?"

"Noodle soup, boss."

"No eggrolls?"

"Eggrolls too."

"Yes, please," the commissaris said.

The food arrived within minutes and the hunchback set the table, taking the rum bottle with him in spite of the captain's protests.

The commissaris stayed another hour, listening to the captain's tales. He heard about the ports of Venezuela and Colombia and there was a long story about Guajira, the peninsula between the two countries where smugglers rule and where Indians still live the Indian life. He was told about the many islands, about revolutions, about sudden gales.

"I nearly lost my first mate then," the captain said, "Maria's brother. How is he, by the way?"

"Her brother?" the commissaris asked, "but she only has sisters."

The captain was trying to light a soggy cigar and, after several attempts, threw it out of the porthole and selected a fresh one from the tin which the commissaris had put on the table.

"Different mother," he said, "but the same father. Maria's father has a lot of children but he was very fond of this son. His mother had come out from Holland to teach here. De Sousa looked after her when she became pregnant and built her a little house in the South. Maria knew her brother, they would come and play on this ship sometimes. The boy went to high school in Amsterdam and later graduated from the merchant navy college. Then he came back."

"You knew him well?" the commissaris asked.

"Of course. He sailed under me for several years. Poor fellow."

"Poor fellow?"

"Yes." The captain stamped on the floor three times.

"Captain?" the hunchback's voice came from the lower deck.

"Can I have that bottle back now?"

"No," the hunchback shouted, "but you can have a beer."

"Beer!" the captain shouted.

Two tins arrived and the captain shoved one to the commissaris. They pulled them open.

"Health."

"The poor fellow," the commissaris reminded him.

"Yes. Natural child, you know. He had his mother's name. His mother married and she didn't have much time for her first child. He hated his father. And he is a small chap, small chaps have a difficult time. He looks small too, some small chaps don't look small but he does. Became very Christian, Bible and all. And then he wouldn't stay with me anymore, he couldn't put up with the drinking and goings on, used to lock himself in his cabin at times. I couldn't help him. But he was a good seaman, I liked him."

"So where is he now?"

"He went back to Holland. Surely you know. Didn't you run into him when Maria got killed?"

"No."

"He is on Schiermonnikoog, 'The Eye of the Gray Monk.' Funny name, that's why I remembered it. He gave up the sea but he had to stay close to it so he picked an island to live on. He became a ranger on a nature reserve. Always liked birds and plants."

"What's his name?" the commissaris asked.

"He has his father's first name and his mother's surname. Ramon Scheffer."

"Thank you," the commissaris said.

14

It was close to four o'clock and still dark. Adjutant Buisman had forced their small dinghy onto the muddy beach.

"This is as close as we can get," he said in a low voice. "You better take off your boots, they'll get stuck in the mud, it's easier if we walk barefoot."

Grijpstra stared at the inky water, de Gier had already pulled off his short boots.

"Ah well," Grijpstra said, more to himself than to anyone else. He found it hard to move in his oilcloth suit and the souwester had tipped into his eyes. With a grunt he managed to get out of his boots and he lowered one foot carefully. It looked very white in the dim early morning light.

The water was cold, about as cold as he had expected it to be.

"Arrrgh," he said in a loud voice as his foot sank into the thick mud.

"Sssh," the adjutant whispered, "the birds. We don't want to disturb them."

"Birds," Grijpstra mumbled. He felt the mud ooze between his toes.

"Bah," he whispered to de Gier, "are you sure this is mud?"

"What else could it be?"

"Dogshit," Grijpstra said.

De Gier laughed politely. He was having his own troubles with the mud which sucked at his legs.

"Careful with the binoculars," the adjutant whispered to Grijpstra. "If we don't bring them back my sergeant will be very upset. He has only just got them."

"Yes, yes," Grijpstra said, and began to wade toward the shore. The dinghy appeared to be sitting on a small bank for the water continued for another fifty yards.

Grijpstra tried not to think as he waded, he only wanted to get to the shore. His foot struck an empty tin and he stumbled but succeeded in staying on his legs. He was the last to arrive.

"Wipe the mud off your feet," the adjutant said, offering Grijpstra a handful of grass. "What happened to your foot? It's bleeding."

De Gier sat down on his haunches and studied Grijpstra's foot. "A wound," he said.

Grijpstra looked down but all he could see was his wide oilcloth trousers.

"Let's go a little farther," de Gier said. "There's some dry sand over there. I've got a torch."

The wound was fairly deep and de Gier cleaned and bandaged it. "Bad luck. Try and walk on it."

Grijpstra could still walk. They put on their socks and shoes again.

"Aha," the adjutant said. "It's getting light now, this is the best time. Look!"

Grijpstra looked and saw a bird, followed by another.

"Plovers," the adjutant exclaimed, adjusting his field glasses.

Grijpstra obediently looked, lifting the heavy binoculars. He saw a blur and felt too cold and too tired to try to adjust the glasses. De Gier saw nothing, he hadn't taken the protecting caps off. The adjutant told him about it.

"Ah yes," de Gier said.

He saw the two small birds.

"Plovers," the adjutant said again. "There are quite a few of them here now, more than last year. Lovely birds. Graceful! Watch them run! They aren't afraid, if they were they would fly. This is a reserve, they know we won't harm them."

Grijpstra moved and his trousers squeaked.

"That's bad," the adjutant said, "can't you take them off? The squeak will irritate the birds. Look! A redshank."

"Where?" Grijpstra asked, feeling that he had to show interest.

"I don't know," de Gier said, "all I can see is a fat yellowshank."

The adjutant had moved away. Grijpstra suddenly turned around and de Gier, startled by Grijpstra's looming shadow, staggered back.

"Cut it out, will you. *You* got me these saffron monstrosities."

"But they are all right, aren't they? They are waterproof. It has begun to rain."

"So it has," Grijpstra said.

It drizzled but Buisman's enthusiasm increased. There were birds everywhere around them and he reeled off their names, telling his guests about the birds' habits.

"Oystercatchers! They can break open the thickest shell with those strong red beaks. Look."

Grijpstra and de Gier looked.

They looked for several hours, staggering about, too tired to lift up their binoculars, gazing dutifully at the busy shapes of seagulls and seemingly endless varieties of duck.

"Eggs," Buisman whispered every now and then. "Be careful! There are a lot of nests about."

"Fried eggs," Grijpstra whispered to de Gier, who had hidden behind a tree, trying to smoke and shielding his cigarette from the rain.

"Fried eggs, and bacon, and tomatoes, and toast."

"Coffee," de Gier said. "We should have brought a thermos flask. I always forget the most important things. Hot coffee!"

"Tell me," Grijpstra said confidentially, "why did we come? Tell me, de Gier, I have forgotten."

"I don't know. We are birdwatchers."

"But why?" Grijpstra insisted. "I don't like birds. Do you?"

"Yes. But not so many of them. This must be their house. They live here. What's that?"

A bird had flown at them and de Gier ducked. There was a rustle of wings and an angry aggressive squeak.

"A peewit," the adjutant, who had been looking for them, suddenly said at Grijpstra's elbow. "Very clever bird. He probably has a nest close by. Look at him now."

The peewit was running about in the grass, one wing dangling to the ground.

"He must have broken his wing on de Gier's head," Grijpstra said admiringly.

"No," Adjutant Buisman said, "he is only pretending. He wants us to go after him. He wants us to think that he is hurt and that he is an easy prey, but he'll fly off as soon as we get too close. His nest will be on the other side."

"Tricky bird, hey?" de Gier said.

Grijpstra didn't agree. If the bird runs on the left the nest is on the right. Easy to remember. He was feeling very hungry now.

"Peewit's eggs are supposed to be a delicacy," he said to Buisman.

"Not now, too late in the year. You should have been

here about a month ago. The first peewit's egg was found here, we sent it to the queen.''

They went on. Grijpstra's mind had sunk into a gray bog. It didn't register anymore. He moved mechanically without noticing that his feet were wet and that the wound on his right big toe was throbbing. He had forgotten his headache and even his hungry feeling had stopped. He no longer pretended any interest but hung behind. He had lost his souwester, the branch of a tree had lifted it off his head and it hung above the path, half a mile behind him, as a gay little flag in an endless wet green maze.

''This is a nice spot,'' Buisman said, and sat down on a log. He opened the gray canvas bag which was strapped to his back and produced a flask of coffee and some cheese rolls. The thermos wasn't big and they only had a sip each. Grijpstra chewed his roll. His bowels rumbled.

''There wouldn't be a toilet anywhere?'' he asked.

''No,'' Buisman said merrily, ''this is pure nature, we are quite a few miles from civilization. But go ahead, go behind those trees over there.''

''Paper,'' Grijpstra mumbled, ''I have no paper.''

''Use some grass. Finest toilet paper in the world.''

''Grass,'' Grijpstra said, and stumped off.

De Gier was grinning when Grijpstra came back.

''All right?''

''Wonderful,'' Grijpstra said. ''There are a lot of birds behind that tree. Look like chickens. Got away from a farm, I guess. I was almost sitting on top of them but they didn't seem to notice. They were stamping around each other.''

Buisman gave a cry of joy and darted at the trees. He was back immediately, waving both arms.

''Fantastic,'' he shouted, ''come and look. Little woodcocks dancing around a hen. I have only seen it once before.''

''I saw them already,'' Grijpstra muttered and refused to budge but de Gier went to see the spectacle.

"Do you see the way they dance?" the adjutant asked.
"It's half aggression half fright, just like us when we make
up to a woman. They are performing, you see, trying to
impress the hen, but she won't look up, she's scratching
away at the ground. If she looks up she has made her
choice and whatever cock she looks at will be her mate.
The others will go away."

De Gier, in spite of the wet cold and his general feeling
of discomfort, was impressed. The cocks had set up the
feathers of their throats and their little combs were upright,
swollen with color.

"A silly show," he said to himself, "but good, in a
way. Like the parties at the police school. All dressed up in
your best uniform and one-two-three, around and around
we go and when she looks at you you can kiss her at her
door."

Grijpstra was alone in the clearing when the little man
appeared.

"Morning," the little man said.

"Morning."

"Birdwatching, are you?"

"I was," Grijpstra said.

"This is a reserve, you know, I am afraid I'll have to ask
you to leave. The birds shouldn't be disturbed, especially
not at this time of the year."

Grijpstra noticed that the little man was wearing some
sort of uniform. He carried a shotgun and there was a
feather in the band of his green hat.

"We are guests of Adjutant Buisman," he said pleasantly.

"Buisman? Is he around?"

"Behind those trees, watching some chickens."

The little man disappeared behind the trees and came
back with Buisman and de Gier.

"Let me introduce my friend," Buisman said, "Rammy Scheffer. He is one of the rangers of the island."

They shook hands and Scheffer sat down. He also had a

flask of coffee, about twice the size of Buisman's flask, and Grijpstra began to think kindly once the hot fluid had activated his stomach, which no longer felt like a shriveled nut.

Buisman and Scheffer began a conversation which seemed to consist mostly of birds' names and de Gier joined Grijpstra on his wet log.

"Seven o'clock," he said. "We could ask them to have breakfast with us."

"Yes," Grijpstra said in a loud voice, "breakfast. Buisman, why don't you and your friend come to the hotel with us? We would like you to have breakfast with us."

Scheffer looked up. "Very kind of you," he said, "but I am on duty. Anyway, we just had coffee. I have some bread and cheese with me and a sausage. You can share it with me if you like."

"Well . . ." Grijpstra began but he was too late. Scheffer had opened his bag and was cutting the bread. He was using a long thin knife.

Buisman was also looking at the knife and he suddenly got up and walked over to Grijpstra, tapping him on the shoulder as he passed him. He kept on going and Grijpstra got up and followed him. When they were out of earshot Buisman cleared his throat.

"I say," he said. "I'd forgotten all about yesterday. I made some inquiries about people who can throw knives but I got nowhere. But now, while I was watching Rammy Scheffer and that nasty-looking knife he has, I have remembered again. I do believe *he* can throw a knife. We have been out together on my boat, years ago now, and he threw a knife at the door of my cabin. I remember now because it annoyed me at the time. He was showing off but it was *my* door which got damaged."

"Yes," Grijpstra said. "What about this fellow? Do you know anything about him?"

"Of course. We all know about each other on the

island. He has been here several years now, three years, I think. He used to be an officer in the merchant navy and he settled here. He is a quiet chap, lives by himself in a little house. He bought it. He has a boat and he sails around the island sometimes. Occasionally he goes to the other shore and stays away for a few days. He doesn't talk much. He was born in Curaçao, hasn't got a police record.''

"Friends? Relatives?"

"Not that I know of. People like him on the island and everybody greets him but he has no special friends. Keeps to himself and reads the Bible, I think. Bit of a fanatic. Grows his own vegetables and bakes his own bread. One of these nature-health people. Doesn't drink, doesn't smoke. Objects to swearing and dirty words. The kids used to tease him, would follow him around mumbling four letter words but we stopped it.''

"Curaçao," Grijpstra mumbled.

"Pardon?"

"Curaçao," Grijpstra repeated. "Our murdered lady came from Curaçao.''

"We could ask him to come over to the station for questioning," Buisman said. "But I would rather not. It's a small island, you know, he'll probably avoid me forever after.''

"Yes," Grijpstra said. "We could ask the commissaris to invite him by letter or send a car for him. If we do it he will connect us with you.''

A siren tore the silence around them to shreds. It seemed very close.

The adjutant stopped. "A siren," he exclaimed. "That's the police launch. They must be trying to find me.''

He began to run. Grijpstra ran after him. They were close to the beach and they reached it within a few minutes. Buisman jumped up and down and waved his arms and a responding movement was seen on the vessel. A rubber dinghy was lowered from the launch and a uniformed policeman rowed to the shore.

Buisman took off his boots and waded into the sea. Grijpstra sighed and followed him. Again he suffered the unpleasant sensation of thick mud oozing between his toes.

"Morning, adjutant," the sergeant in the dinghy said to Buisman.

He shook Grijpstra's hand.

"Grijpstra, Amsterdam police."

"Good," the sergeant said. "I have a Telex for you. An urgent Telex. I knew the adjutant was out here with you this morning. Here you are."

Grijpstra read the Telex.

"Go to Schiermonnikoog at once and make contact with Ramon Scheffer. Scheffer is half-brother of Maria van Buren. Caution important. Scheffer is said to be religious fanatic."

The Telex was dated a day back, came from Curaçao, was forwarded by Amsterdam Headquarters and was signed by the commissaris.

15

"HERE YOU ARE," Rammy Scheffer said, and de Gier thanked him and bit into the thick slice of bread. He chewed for a while.

"Do you like the cheese?" Rammy asked.

"Yes," de Gier said hesitantly, and continued to chew.

"What is it?"

"Goat's cheese. I have got two goats, milk them myself."

De Gier chewed on for a while.

"Ah," he said. "I say! Over there! What's that bird?"

Rammy looked and de Gier took the cheese off the bread and threw it into a bush. He quickly stuffed the bread into his mouth.

"That's an oystercatcher," Rammy said, looking back at de Gier. "Didn't you know? There are thousands of them on the island. Apart from the gulls and the ducks they are the most popular birds over here."

"I'd forgotten," de Gier said.

"Are you interested in birds?"

"Of course," de Gier said, swallowing the last of his bread and hopefully holding up his cup for more coffee but Rammy's flask was empty.

"Good," Rammy said. "If more people were interested in birds we might succeed in keeping a few around. The way it's going now we'll soon say goodbye to the last of them. They are installing new drainpipes, I hear, as if the sea isn't dirty enough already. Every day I try to clean the beaches of this reserve but there is no end to the plastic bottles and the ice cream cups, and now we'll have industrial dirt as well."

"Yes," de Gier said. "Terrible."

"Your friend, is he a birdwatcher too?"

"Sure," de Gier said.

"He wasn't watching the dance of the cocks. It's a rare sight; even I, who am here everyday, don't see it often."

"He hurt his foot," de Gier said, "ripped his toe on a piece of tin or a broken bottle. I think he wanted to sit and rest a little."

"I see," Rammy said, sliding the strap of the shotgun off his shoulder, and balancing the weapon on his lap.

The siren shrieked and de Gier jumped up. "Hell," he said, "what's that?"

Rammy had jumped as well, staring toward the sea. "A boat," he said, "a boat in trouble perhaps. Ran aground probably. Let's go and see."

He pointed and de Gier began to run.

De Gier arrived at the beach.

"You!" Grijpstra said when he saw de Gier coming out of the bush. "What are you doing here? Where is Rammy?"

De Gier was panting. "Behind me somewhere. Where's the boat?"

"Over there." Grijpstra pointed at the police launch, floating quietly a quarter of a mile offshore.

"What's the matter with her?"

"Nothing," Grijpstra said. "Where is Rammy?"

"How should I know?"

"You lost him?"

De Gier gaped at Grijpstra and the adjutant. The sergeant had reached them as well now.

"Fool," Grijpstra said sadly. "He is the man we want and you had him in your hands."

"What. . . ?" de Gier began and gave up.

"He doesn't know, Grijpstra," Adjutant Buisman said.

"Doesn't know *what*?" de Gier asked.

"Never mind," Grijpstra said, "you are a fool anyway, you *should* have known. Shall we try to follow him, Buisman?"

"No. Rammy knows the reserve better than we do. We may as well sit down somewhere here and think for a while."

"WHAT. . . ?" de Gier began again.

"All right," Buisman said, "show him the Telex, Grijpstra."

De Gier read the Telex, and immediately lost his temper.

"So how should *I* have known he is the man we are looking for. *I* was talking to a little fellow in a green hat who gave me a sandwich. Hey!"

He interrupted himself. "He had a shotgun!"

"So?" Grijpstra asked.

"He could have *shot* me," de Gier said. "He took it off his shoulder while he was talking to me. He suspected something."

"Nonsense," Grijpstra said. "He thought we were birdwatchers."

De Gier stared at Grijpstra.

"Birdwatchers! You weren't watching any birds. You were sitting on a log groaning and mumbling to yourself while the rare cocks were doing their sublime prance. That's what made him suspicious."

"I had watched them already," Grijpstra said. "I was resting. Even birdwatchers rest."

"Yes. And then you sneaked off with Buisman."

"I was telling Grijpstra that Rammy could be his man," Buisman said. "I had remembered that Rammy could throw a knife."

"You see!" de Gier shouted, "and you didn't warn me. You left me sitting with a dangerous murderer holding a *shotgun* in his hands and now you tell me I am a fool."

"Yes," Grijpstra said soothingly, "true. You could have been a dead fool. You should be grateful."

De Gier took a deep breath. The adjutant patted him on the shoulder.

"There, there," Buisman said.

"Oh, never mind him," Grijpstra said, "he always exaggerates."

"Exaggerates?" de Gier shouted.

"Of course," Buisman said, "I have known Rammy Scheffer for years. He isn't a violent man. He proved it, didn't he? He ran away. He could have shot you but he didn't. He didn't even threaten you."

"He threw a knife into his sister's back," de Gier said.

"Perhaps he did. It hasn't been proved."

"Perhaps we should try to catch him," Grijpstra said. "Where can he be? He wouldn't try to hide in this swamp, would he?"

"No," the water-police sergeant who, so far, had contented himself with watching the scene and rolling himself a cigarette, said quietly, "He won't even try to hide on the island. He is a sailor and he has a boat."

"A boat," Grijpstra said, but the rest of his words were drowned in a deafening roar of sudden noise. The noise was above them and still increasing in volume. The four men ducked instinctively.

"They are at it again," the sergeant said when the noise had subsided. The jet fighter was only a speck on the horizon now.

"Fooee," Grijpstra said, "what a racket. Nice quiet island you have here."

"They only do it twice a week now," Buisman said. "Starfighters. They practice all day, shooting their cannon at targets that have been set up for them on the next island. Sometimes they do a bit of bombing as well. They always come over this part of the island. It used to be much worse but our mayor protested to the Air Force."

"You were saying?" de Gier asked.

"Ah yes," Grijpstra said. "Rammy has a boat, the sergeant says, but so have we. There she is. A nice fast police launch. Let's get aboard."

"Which way do you want me to go?" the sergeant said.

"To wherever he parks his boat, of course."

The sergeant shook his head. "I don't know where his boat is. She isn't in the harbor where she should be. He took her out last week. She may be in any of several places now and if he is aboard he may be sailing in a lot of different directions. We would be very lucky if we caught up with him."

"A plane," the adjutant said, "a spotter plane. We have got police planes, haven't we?"

"We could ask a starfighter to do a bit of spotting," de Gier said.

"No," the adjutant said, "they are fools. They fly at a million miles an hour and all they have learned to do is strafe. If we ask them to help us they will dive at every pleasure yacht and at every fishing boat and people will dive overboard and drown and we'll never hear the end of it. The spotter planes are just what we need. Let's get to the launch and raise the airport on the mainland radio."

It wasn't as easy as the adjutant thought. Of the two available police planes one was being serviced. Of the four available pilots one had taken a day off, one had reported sick, and the other two couldn't be found. It took an hour for the plane to take off. The adjutant fretted and the sergeant made coffee. Grijpstra fussed with his pistol, which had jammed. Only de Gier felt happy, he was sitting on the roof of the launch cabin and admiring the view. It was nine o'clock in the morning and the sky was clear with only a few clouds drifting above the island. The star-fighters had disappeared, having been asked by the police of the airport to clear off for a while so as not to bother the spotter plane.

"I thought you were all upset," Grijpstra said. He had managed to get his pistol in working order again and was feeling better.

"I have forgiven you," de Gier said.

"Thanks. Maybe I should have let you know, but he wouldn't have harmed you. You looked too innocent, sitting on that log in your duffelcoat."

"He gave me a piece of goat's cheese," de Gier said.

"Was it nice?"

"Wonderful," de Gier said. "It had a delicate taste. He had made it himself from milk that came from his own goats."

"Sha," Grijpstra said, and shuddered.

"No, really, it was delicious. We get spoiled in the city, you know."

Grijpstra had climbed on the cabin's roof and sat looking around him. He was mumbling.

"Goat's cheese," Grijpstra said. "I suppose he picks stinging nettles and boils soup with them. I have a niece who does that. A nature girl, goes all the way to France to run about naked."

"Good-looking girl?" de Gier asked.

"Not bad," Grijpstra said. "Look, there's our plane."

The spotter plane, a small Piper Cub, was gaining height.

"I could have been a pilot," de Gier said.

"No," Grijpstra interrupted. "Let's not have your fancies today. You might not enjoy it, you know, up there in a mechanical fly. I was in one of them once."

"Yes? What was it like?"

"First I got scared, and later I fell asleep. You can't see much. Too high. You see a lot of green land and little cars."

"Yes," de Gier said. "I have been in a plane. Everybody has. But not in a little plane, don't tell me it wasn't an adventure."

"It wasn't. And the window wouldn't close, there was a draft."

"A draft," de Gier said, and shook his head.

Grijpstra pulled up his legs and clasped his arms around his knees. The sun was beginning to warm them. "Not bad," he said approvingly, "a lot better than all that mud. And those birds, they were really making me nervous. I don't mind them in the zoo, you can always get away from them. Holland was full of birds once, they say, billions of them. The whole country was marshland. Good thing we built dikes and drained the swamps. Imagine, living in a swamp with a billion birds flapping around and diving at you like that ballwit which had a go at you."

"Peewit."

"Peewit. Funny-looking bird. Some of them look all right but I still wouldn't like to live right in the middle of a whole flock of them, in a hut. The old tribes must have lived in huts, they were probably flooded twice a week." Grijpstra sneezed.

"And they had colds," de Gier said, "and diarrhea."

"Yes. So have I. And these damned oilcloth trousers. I couldn't get them off properly."

De Gier began to laugh. Grijpstra turned around, looking hurt.

"Listen," de Gier said.

Adjutant Buisman was talking to the pilot on the radio. "A small yacht," he was saying, "white mainsail and white foresail, only one foresail. The foresail has two patches in it, large patches, you should be able to see them."

"I only see a fishing boat," the pilot said.

"No markings on the yacht's sails. The boat we want is some thirty feet long, built of oak."

"Thanks," the pilot said. "Oak, you say. How do I spot oak from here?"

"Brown wood."

The radio crackled for a while.

"I am going east," the pilot said, "there's nothing this side except a fishing boat and a very expensive looking blue yacht. There is a girl at the rudder, I think. A pretty girl maybe."

"What's your rank?" Buisman asked.

"Sergeant, and yours?"

"Adjutant," Buisman said.

"Adjutant is higher."

"Go east," Buisman said.

"Sir."

"Here," the pilot said after a few minutes. "Small yacht, thirty feet. One man in it, or perhaps there is somebody in the cabin."

"Our man wears a green suit, a ranger's uniform."

"Green suit," the pilot confirmed. "I am very low now, shall I scare him?"

"Turn a few circles," Buisman said. "Can we have his position?"

"Just a minute," the pilot said. "Bring out your map, I am trying to find mine."

The water-police sergeant moved a lever and the launch picked up speed suddenly. Grijpstra began to slide toward de Gier who couldn't hold him and they landed up together on the small afterdeck, next to the sergeant.

"Let us know next time, will you?" Grijpstra said gruffly, picking himself up.

"Sorry," the sergeant said. "I got excited. Maybe we'll have a nice chase."

The launch went into a steep curve and its engine roared.

"Don't get too close," de Gier said. "He's got a shotgun."

"What have we got?" Grijpstra asked.

"I am not armed," Buisman said. "Do you have anything in the launch, sergeant?"

"A carbine, and I have a pistol."

"Three pistols and a carbine against a shotgun," de Gier said. "That should be enough."

The radio had been talking to them but nobody was listening.

"Hello," it shouted.

"Yes, pilot," Buisman said.

"Do you want the position or don't you?"

"Please."

They found the position on their map and the sergeant looked grim. The launch was going at full speed now, planing on the sea's calm surface, its two propellers churning the water behind into deep swirling eddies, its engine going at a steady low roar. De Gier was holding on to the cabin, trying to see everything at the same time and getting so excited that he was having trouble breathing. Buisman was arming the carbine, his eyes contracted into slits, and even Grijpstra felt the sensation of the hunt and was beginning to forget the pain in his lungs and the burning of his bowels.

"Hello," the radio shouted.

"Go ahead," Buisman said.

"He is going to Englishman's Bank," the pilot said. "I can see both of you now but you can't cut him off. He is very close already, his engine is going and he has lowered his mainsail. I'll dive at him."

"No," Buisman shouted, "he has got a shotgun."

"That what it is, is it? He is pointing something at me now."

"Get away," Buisman shouted.

"I have got away. What do you want me to do now?"

The launch was turning around the southern tip of the

island and suddenly they saw both the yacht and the Piper Cub.

"Go home," the adjutant said. "We can see him. I don't think there's anything you can do now."

"O.K.," the pilot said.

"Thanks, sergeant, you've been a great help."

"You are welcome," the radio said. "Out."

"We can't go any faster," the water-police sergeant said, "and he is almost there."

Buisman and Grijpstra were watching the small green figure through their binoculars. Rammy was standing in the bow of his yacht. They saw him jump and land on the sandbank. He was still wearing his hat and holding the shotgun.

The sergeant throttled the engine down until it was merely idling.

"What does he want out there?" the sergeant asked. "The bank is two square miles perhaps and nothing grows on it, not a blade of grass. In four hours time it will be almost flooded. He'll have a few square yards left to run about in."

"He is going to the hut," Buisman said.

They saw the hut, a small cabin built on high poles, thirty feet high. The cabin looked pretty, with a sloping roof, a narrow balcony on all sides, and windows.

"What's that?" de Gier asked.

"It's just there," Buisman said. "Waterworks put it up. I think they may have planned it for a watchman but there's never been a watchman in it as far as I can remember. There's nothing to watch anyway. Seals sometimes sun themselves on the bank, and there are birds, of course."

"It serves some purpose," the sergeant said. "If anyone gets stranded on the bank he can sit in the hut and wait for help. When the sea is very high the bank gets completely flooded but the cabin will always be dry. There's some food up there, emergency rations, and water, and a pistol with flares. I collected a stranded crew once who had spent half a day in it.''

"He is climbing the stairs,'' de Gier said.

Buisman sighed. "You know what he is planning to do, don't you?''

"Yes,'' Grijpstra said.

The sergeant was lowering the anchor.

"You can switch the engine off,'' the adjutant said. "We may be here for some time.''

The four men were looking at each other.

"You,'' Grijpstra said to de Gier. "You sometimes have bright ideas. Now what?''

De Gier grinned. "Wait,'' he said. "What else? He's got food and he's got water and he is armed. When we get too close he'll spend a couple of shells on us. With the carbine we could probably outshoot him but he has some cover in there and we'll be on the open bank. And it wouldn't be nice, popping away at him. We'll have to starve him out, taking turns. We can probably get some men from the mainland to relieve us.'' He looked at the sergeant. "You'll have to get back to the island, do you have somebody out there?''

"Riekers,'' the sergeant said. "He is the only policeman on the island now and he can't be everywhere at the same time. We are supposed to meet the ferries and patrol the camps. There are a few hundred tourists out there and some hippies, and nine hundred islanders. We can't spend all day here.''

"We can try and talk to him,'' Grijpstra said, looking at Buisman.

"Do you know him well, sergeant?'' Buisman asked.

The water-police sergeant scratched his neck. "Well, I have talked to him, of course, but we aren't close friends. He isn't an easy man to get along with. He doesn't drink.''

"No,'' Buisman agreed, "and when he talks it's Bible talk. Old Testament.''

"The God of vengeance," de Gier said, "Jehovah."

"Jehovah wasn't easy to get on with either," Grijpstra said. "Well, as you say, we can't sit here all day. If you lower that dinghy, sergeant, I'll row myself ashore and see if I can get close to him. He won't kill me in cold blood."

"No," de Gier said, "I'll go. I can pull my gun faster than you can. I won second prize at the rifle range last week. If he does grab his shotgun I can shoot him in the arm perhaps."

"Lower the dinghy, sergeant," Buisman said in a low voice. "I'll go. I do know him after all."

Grijpstra protested and the sergeant offered to go but Buisman insisted.

The three men watched the dinghy approach the bank.

"Look," de Gier said, and pointed at the cabin on stilts. Rammy Scheffer had appeared on the balcony.

Buisman was clambering out of the dinghy, being careful not to upset it. They saw him walking to the cabin and they saw Rammy shouldering the shotgun. Buisman stopped. He was shouting through cupped hands. De Gier saw Rammy shake his head slowly. They heard the deep bark of the shotgun.

Buisman was still on his feet. They saw him turn around. He was holding his chest and staggering.

"The bastard," the sergeant said, pumping up a second dinghy furiously. De Gier took the carbine and the two of them gingerly boarded the small rubber boat.

The sergeant was a skillfull rower and the dinghy shot through the small waves which a weak breeze had begun to form. They reached the bank in minutes and de Gier shouldered the carbine. He missed Rammy Scheffer deliberately but the bullet struck the cabin close to his head and Rammy disappeared into the cabin.

"Run," de Gier shouted at the sergeant as he fired at the cabin, hitting it just under the roof. The adjutant was still on his feet but moving slowly. The sergeant sprinted and picked Buisman up, talking to him softly.

"You'll be all right, Buisman, hold on to my neck."

De Gier fired once more but there was no sign of either Rammy or his weapon.

"Never mind now," the sergeant said. "He can't hit us here. I'll take Buisman and you can take the other dinghy. Can you row?"

"Yes," de Gier said.

The two dinghies got to the launch at the same time and Grijpstra helped the sergeant to get Buisman aboard. Together they opened his coat. The fine shot had drawn a lot of blood but the wounds weren't deep. Buisman's jacket had protected him somewhat. He hadn't been hurt in the face.

"You deal with it," the sergeant said. "I'll see if we can get help."

The island didn't answer. The sergeant kept on trying.

"Riekers must have left the station," the sergeant muttered. "He is probably trying to find us. He could have called me, the idiot."

"You were on another frequency," de Gier said, "talking to the plane."

"True," the sergeant said. "Now what? We can't leave that murdering rat alone, he'll escape in his boat."

"We can take his boat with us, can't we?"

"No," the sergeant said, "he may swim off the bank. He is a good swimmer."

A jetfighter came screaming over, throwing its shadow at them and drowning them in noise.

"When you have had everything," de Gier said when the airplane had disappeared.

"The jets," Grijpstra suddenly shouted. "*Now* they can help."

De Gier and the sergeant looked at Grijpstra.

"Don't you understand?" Grijpstra shouted. "Get them on the radio and tell them to fly at that cabin. They'll scare him out in no time at all."

"Genius," de Gier said.

The sergeant was on the radio again.

"Can you get the fighter base for me, sir?"

"Why?" a gruff voice answered.

The sergeant explained. He had to explain several times.

"Very irregular," the gruff voice said.

"Rather an irregular situation, sir," the sergeant said.

"How is your adjutant?"

"Needs medical help."

"All right," the voice said. "We'll send you a boat with a doctor. It will take an hour, two hours maybe, and I'll telephone the island and tell them to send your doctor out as well, in somebody's yacht. And I'll speak to the fighter base about this. I'll probably get into trouble but that'll be later. Out."

The first jet appeared within five minutes. It circled to make sure of its target, climbed and roared down. The men in the boat were covering their ears and trying to get as low down as possible. De Gier suddenly stopped regretting that he had never been in a war. The immense whine of the jet chilled his body and made tears spring to his eyes. He forced himself to keep his eyes open and he saw the plane grow in size until it was blotting out the sky. Then he turned his head and saw the fighter skim the cabin's roof with seemingly no more than a few feet to spare. When he looked around again the second fighter entered its dive while the first was climbing and going into a bank to regain its original position. The second fighter got even closer to the cabin's roof than the first.

The radio was muttering and the sergeant turned up the volume.

"Are they there?" the police officer on the mainland was asking.

"Just listen, sir," the sergeant said, and held the mi-

crophone above his head as the first fighter came screaming down again.

"They aren't firing their guns, are they?" the voice
asked.

"No, sir, just diving."

"It sounds like the end of the world."

"Here the other one comes again," the sergeant said.

"That's it," de Gier shouted.

They saw the green-clad figure of Rammy appearing on
the balcony. He was waving his hands. He didn't have the
shotgun. "Come down," de Gier shouted, forgetting that
Rammy couldn't hear him.

Rammy was coming down, he was falling down the
staircase in his hurry to reach the ground. They saw him
running toward them. The jetfighters had seen him too and
they stopped diving and began to circle.

De Gier grabbed the carbine and lowered himself into a
dinghy.

"Wait," Grijpstra shouted, and put his leg over the side
of the launch.

Grijpstra rowed while de Gier covered Rammy with his
carbine. Rammy was waiting for them, quietly, his arms
dangling down. When they came close they saw that his
mouth was open and that spittle was trickling down its
corners.

"Put your hands up," de Gier said in a loud voice,
thinking of the long knife which would be somewhere
under the green jacket, but Rammy didn't hear him.

Grijpstra walked around the prisoner and patted his
jacket. He found the knife and put it away. The handcuffs
clicked. Rammy began to mutter.

"What's he saying?" de Gier asked Grijpstra.

Rammy's voice was very low and Grijpstra bent his
head trying to catch the meaning of the words.

"I don't know," he said after a while, "something
about Satan."

"Come with us, Rammy," de Gier said gently. "Nobody is going to harm you. Just get into the dinghy and we'll go to the launch. Soon you will have a nice sleep."

Rammy looked up.

"You'll be fine," Grijpstra said.

16

"YOU ARE not too badly hurt," the doctor said, "but you are hurt. How is the pain?"

"All right," Buisman said, and groaned.

"I'll have to get that shot out of your chest. Most of it sits in your clothes but there's some in your skin as well. We can take you to the mainland and keep you in hospital for a while."

"No."

"You prefer to go home?"

"Please," Buisman said. "The food is better."

The doctor nodded and turned toward the shape of Rammy, who was sitting on the floorboards of the launch. He was shaking and his teeth were chattering.

"How are you, Rammy?" the doctor asked.

The doctor touched his head, very lightly, but the small ranger didn't notice.

"Shock," the doctor said to de Gier. "Bad shock. He'll have to go to the mainland. You want to come with us?"

De Gier didn't answer but looked down at Rammy Scheffer.

"How bad is he, doctor?"

"Bad."

"Where will you take him?"

"To a mental home," the doctor said.

"Yes?" de Gier asked, surprised. "That bad?"

They had walked over to the other side of the launch and were leaning over the railing, watching the sea, as the launch returned to the island's harbor. The little private yacht which had brought the doctor was following them at a hundred yards' distance.

"Yes," the doctor said, "his mind is shaken all right. I have known Rammy ever since he came to the island. He lived under stress. He is a regular patient of mine."

"What was the matter with him?"

"Ulcers, and other nervous complaints. Breathing trouble, he often thought he would choke. Once he came in the middle of the night, holding his throat. Told me I had to operate straightaway."

"What was it?" de Gier asked. "Asthma?"

"Nothing I could diagnose," the doctor said.

"So?"

"I recommended a psychiatrist."

"Did he go to see one?"

"No."

"What do you think was the matter with him?"

"No," the doctor said, "that's all I will tell you. Perhaps the psychiatrist in the mental home I'll take him to will say more. But you can't arrest him, that's for sure. You'll have to take the handcuffs off. I'll give him something to keep him calm and the police launch can take us to the mainland. I'll go with him. You want to come?"

"Not unless you want me to," de Gier said.

They stood in silence for a while.

"Will you do me a favor?" de Gier suddenly asked.

"Certainly."

"Look at my mate," de Gier said. "I think he is ill."

They found Grijpstra in the bow of the launch.

"Nice day," the doctor said.

Grijpstra turned around, trying to smile. His face was covered with sweat.

"I am a bit seasick," he said. "It'll pass. I was sick on the ferry yesterday."

"Yes," the doctor said, "you have my sympathy. I get seasick myself, but not on small boats. I went on a cruise once, with my wife, two weeks on the Mediterranean. I was sick most of the time."

Grijpstra smiled. The doctor had a pleasant way of talking.

"Do you mind if I feel your pulse?"

Grijpstra offered his arm, and began to cough.

"He has influenza, doctor," de Gier said, "and he has the shits as well."

Grijpstra stopped coughing and glared at de Gier.

"He should be in bed," de Gier said.

Grijpstra sneezed.

"Your friend is right," the doctor said. "You aren't just seasick. You'll have to go to bed right away."

"Bed?" Grijpstra asked. "Why?"

"Why?" de Gier said. "Look at him. You probably have pneumonia and dysentery."

"Why don't you take me to the cemetery?" Grijpstra asked. "And why don't you mind your own business?"

"No," the doctor said, "don't get upset. I am a doctor and I say you are ill. Not very ill, but ill. And you'll have to go to bed."

"I'll go back to Amsterdam," Grijpstra said. "I'll be all right. It's all this nature."

"You can't go to Amsterdam," de Gier said, and turned. He found Buisman in the cabin, stretched out on a bench. The water-police sergeant had made him as comfortable as he could, putting him on a thin mattress and covering him up with a blanket.

"How do you feel?" de Gier asked.

"Terrible," Buisman said, "but I'll feel a lot better

when I see my wife. She used to be a nurse and she cooks well. I could do with a few days in bed.''

"Grijpstra is ill,'' de Gier said.

"Good.''

"What do you mean?'' de Gier asked, raising his voice.

"I'll have some company,'' Buisman said. "We can play cards and talk to each other.''

"Your wife won't mind?''

"No,'' Buisman said. "She likes to be a nurse.''

"I don't think he'll play cards with you,'' de Gier said. "he has influenza and dysentery.''

"Is that what the doctor says?''

"The doctor says he is ill.''

"He'll be all right,'' Buisman said. "You don't know my wife.''

"It's all fixed,'' de Gier said. "You are going to stay in Buisman's house. His wife is a nurse and she cooks well.''

"Right,'' the doctor said.

Grijpstra wanted to say something but sneezed instead.

A crowd was waiting for them in the island's harbor and de Gier studied it through his binoculars. He saw the commissaris and IJsbrand Drachtsma. He waved at the commissaris, who put up a hand. The commissaris was still wearing his shantung suit. He hadn't been home; a police car had taken him from Amsterdam airport to the Schiermonnikoog ferry. He had only just arrived. He was talking to Mr. Drachtsma, and de Gier, although he realized it was rude to stare at the two men, kept his binoculars steady. Drachtsma was answering the commissaris now. He spoke at length.

The launch touched the quay, and moored. Another similar launch was moored close by. Policemen from the mainland helped de Gier carry Rammy Scheffer. The handcuffs were taken off and Rammy was made to swallow a pill. The chattering and shaking stopped but the small ranger's eyes were still without any expression.

The island doctor spoke to the doctor the launch had brought. De Gier introduced the two doctors to the commissaris. Buisman was carried ashore on a stretcher and de Gier supported Grijpstra, who had stopped pretending and who now accepted help. A local car offered to take the two policemen to Buisman's house. Buisman's wife, a fat kindly-looking woman, went with them.

De Gier felt a hand on his shoulder and looked around.

"Right," the commissaris said, "let's have some coffee somewhere. You got my cable, I see."

17

THEY HAD coffee, they had lunch, they had more coffee, and then they had some brandy.

"Well," the commissaris said finally, when de Gier, now very relaxed and smiling, had finally stopped talking.

"So you two would have found him anyway."

"Perhaps not," de Gier said.

"Yes, you would have found him."

"No, sir. I am not sure. The siren of the police launch shook him. And it was you who sent the launch, she came to bring your Telex."

"Yes, perhaps."

The commissaris smiled. "I wouldn't have minded if you had found him on your own. The trip to Curaçao was a good trip."

"What happened?" de Gier asked.

They had more brandy. The afternoon passed as the commissaris talked.

"But why?" the commissaris asked, "why think of Drachtsma?"

They were walking toward Buisman's house and the rain had started again. The commissaris had no raincoat and they were walking quickly.

"Let's go into the hotel, sir, we can go later, or telephone. Perhaps we should go tomorrow."

"All right, I'll book into the hotel. Why Drachtsma?"

"He is a powerful man," de Gier said, struggling out of his duffelcoat.

"Yes," the commissaris said.

They sat down in de Gier's room and the commissaris rubbed his legs.

"How are your legs, sir?"

"They hurt again. They didn't hurt in Curaçao. I'll have a hot bath later."

The commissaris stretched out on the bed that Grijpstra had used.

"IJsbrand Drachtsma is a powerful man."

"Yes," de Gier said, "and Maria van Buren was a powerful woman."

"I see," the commissaris said. "He wanted to own her and she was manipulating him. A conflict of interest. It might be a motive."

"She was a sorcerer, a witch," de Gier said. "You found her master. What was he like?"

"I told you," the commissaris said. "I never found out what he was like. I fell asleep on his porch and I left when I woke up. He was very kind to me."

"Perhaps he was a *good* sorcerer," de Gier said. "Magic goes both ways, doesn't it."

"Yes. I thought about that too. She was his disciple. She learned from him. She got some power."

"And she used it the other way around."

"All right, all right," the commissaris said. "She put a spell on Drachtsma. The big tycoon, the president of companies, the hero-soldier, the sportsman, the intellectual, the leader. And she had him on a string. So he killed her."

"Yes," de Gier said.

"But he couldn't have," the commissaris said. "He had an alibi. I checked his alibi. I spoke to the German police. The two men who confirmed that they spent that Saturday with him, all day and all evening, are respectable men. Drachtsma was in Schiermonnikoog when Maria caught the knife in her back."

De Gier lit a cigarette and walked over to the window. "Perhaps Drachtsma learned some sorcery as well," de Gier said.

The commissaris sat up, looking at de Gier's back.

"He used Rammy Scheffer, you mean," he said.

De Gier didn't answer.

"Could be," the commissaris said slowly. "Rammy Scheffer is a mentally disturbed man. He dropped out of the merchant navy. He hates his father. His father didn't marry his mother. And he loved his sister."

"Jehovah," de Gier muttered.

"The Bible," the commissaris said. "Have you read the Bible, de Gier?"

"Yes. At Sunday school. I know some of the Old Testament by heart."

"The Bible is an interesting book," the commissaris said.

De Gier turned around quickly. "A very dangerous book, sir."

"If it is read the wrong way."

"I saw a German army belt once," de Gier said. "Somebody had kept it as a souvenir of the war. It had some words on the clasp. GOTT MIT UNS."

"God with us," the commissaris said.

"The SS soldiers wore those belts too," de Gier said. "They killed six million Jews."

"Yes," the commissaris said slowly, "so Drachtsma played on the feelings of Maria's half brother. He told him that Satan had got into her and had made her his vehicle."

"Hard to prove," de Gier said.

"Impossible to prove. But we could satisfy our curiosity. We could go and see Drachtsma."

"Hc was talking to you on the quay, wasn't he, sir?"

"Yes," the commissaris said, "and he was very nervous. He kept on talking, I couldn't get a word in edgewise once he got started."

"Was he saying anything?"

"No. He was asking what I thought. If I thought that poor fellow had done it. He said he knew him well and that Rammy is mentally unstable."

"Did you tell him that Rammy Scheffer was Maria van Buren's half brother?"

"Yes."

"And?"

"He said he didn't know."

18

IT WAS FIVE O'CLOCK in the afternoon and the commissaris was about to lower himself into the bath when the telephone in his room began to ring.

"This is Drachtsma."

The commissaris mumbled something, trying to hold on to the towel which was slipping off his narrow hips.

"I thought that you would perhaps stay on the island until tomorrow and I was wondering if you would care to join us for dinner tonight. The island's mayor is coming as well and some of the aldermen and I thought that you might like to meet them."

"Thank you," the commissaris said, trying to light a cigar and hold on to the towel at the same time. "Would you mind if I brought my assistant, Sergeant de Gier? I don't think he'll enjoy having dinner by himself and Adjutant Grijpstra is ill and staying with the Buismans' for the time being."

There was a short silence. "I don't know whether the sergeant will feel comfortable in the presence of tonight's company."

The commissaris bit on his cigar, it broke, and he spat it out.

"I am sure he'll be *quite* comfortable."

"All right," Drachtsma said. "The sergeant will be welcome. I wonder if you could come between seven and seven-thirty? Shall I send the car for you?"

"I have seen your house, somebody pointed it out to me. It couldn't be more than a few miles from the hotel. I think we'll walk."

"See you tonight," Drachtsma said.

"Bah," the commissaris said, lit a fresh cigar, picked up the towel, and marched into the bathroom.

De Gier was telephoning to Headquarters in Amsterdam.

"We have got him," he was saying to Adjutant Geurts, "a half-brother of the murdered woman. Family drama, very sad."

"Did he confess?"

"No, he went mad instead."

"But you are sure he did it?"

"He threw the knife," de Gier said.

"Congratulations. What about this Mr. Holman, the fellow with the red waistcoat? He is due to come to see us again tonight. We had him here yesterday as well."

"No, he is all right," de Gier said.

"I am not so sure. He is very nervous, you know, he must be hiding something or other."

"Probably hasn't paid enough tax," de Gier said. "Phone him and tell him we have found our man."

"All right," Adjutant Geurts said. "Give me a ring when you get to Amsterdam, I'll meet you somewhere for a drink. Sietsema and I would like to hear all about it."

"No, not tonight. We aren't finished yet, and Grijpstra is ill. It may be a few days."

"What do you mean 'not finished'? You have your man, haven't you?"

"Yes, yes," de Gier said, "but it's a funny case."

"And Grijpstra? What's wrong with him?"

"Flu. I'll go and see him now, he is staying with friends."

"You are having a holiday," Geurts said. "I know. Sitting on the beach."

"Yes," de Gier said, "and we are allowed to use the police launch. And there is a yacht. And I have met some girls. We are going to a party tonight. A wild party. The island is full of naturalists. We'll be chasing each other on the beach tonight, stark naked. It's full moon, you know. These islands are different from what we are used to on the mainland. People are very free. The girls will come up to you and smile and say 'would you like to sleep with me tonight?' and nobody minds. Not even their husbands or boyfriends. And they have some beautiful folk dances."

"Really?"

"Yes," de Gier said.

"Do they still do headhunting?"

"They drink beer from the skulls of their enemies and wear rabbit skins. But I'll have to ring off."

"Bah," Geurts said to Sietsema who had been listening in. "Have you noticed it always happens to them? Nothing ever happens to us."

"Never mind," Sietsema said. "We still have that old lady who was clobbered on the head by the two Arabs and the man who has a houseful of stolen bicycles. And another case came up this afternoon while you were in the canteen. It sounds interesting."

"What case?"

"A man who was taken to hospital this morning by ambulance. He has cracked his skull and broken his arm and there is something wrong with his leg. He told an unlikely story to the doctor and the doctor didn't believe him and phoned us."

"What story?"

"Well," Sietsema said, looking through his notes. "I hope I have got it right. The man is a student who lives in a garden flat, that's a beautified cellar, I believe. He often sleeps late and this morning he only got up at eleven because somebody rang his bell. He was still groggy from last night's drinking and he didn't bother to dress so he was walking through the corridor without his clothes. The bell was still ringing and he began to run and his cat, a young playful animal, jumped up and took a swing at his balls. But the cat had forgotten to keep his nails in and he really got the man."

"Ha."

"Yes," Sietsema said, "so the man jumped up and cracked his skull on a pipe, a gas pipe running along the ceiling. Somebody saw him lying in the corridor. He was bleeding and he had hurt his foot when he fell. The ambulance came and the attendants strapped him to the stretcher. He was still conscious so they asked him what happened and he told them. And then they laughed so much that they dropped the stretcher and he broke his arm."

Geurts stared at Sergeant Sietsema. "You are getting like de Gier," he said.

"No. Here is the number. Ring the hospital. They reckon it can't be true and that someone must have beaten him up."

Geurts picked up the telephone.

De Gier was walking on the island's main dike. It was low tide and a sea of mud stretched on for miles. Thousands of birds were feeding in the mud and their white bodies contrasted with the dark clouds packed on the horizon. The island's people were all in their houses having tea, and the world around him was quiet; not even the birds made a sound, being too busy with their feeding. He stopped and gazed. A horse, tied to a stake in a meadow on the other side of the dike, whinnied. De Gier looked at the horse. The sun, shining through a hole in the clouds, seemed to concentrate on the horse and it looked as if it had been set alight, a white burning horse prancing about in the dark green meadow. De Gier sighed.

He looked up at the clouds. The hole was closing and there was only one beam of orange light left, but it was still focused on the horse which, as if it felt that it was being part of the inexpressible, reared and shook its forelegs.

"Good day, Mrs. Buisman," de Gier said. "How are your patients?"

"Come in and have some tea," the fat woman said, looking efficient in her white apron. "Your friend is fast asleep. But he is ill. You were right. He does have pneumonia and his temperature is high. He may be here for quite a while but he should feel better soon, maybe even by tomorrow."

"Good. And your husband?"

"The shot has been taken out of his chest. It was easy fortunately, but his skin is broken in a lot of places."

"Good thing he wasn't hit in the face."

"Rammy wouldn't have hit him in the face," Mrs. Buisman said. "He was only trying to stop my husband from arresting him, poor fellow."

"Poor fellow," de Gier muttered. "He killed his sister, you know."

Mrs. Buisman poured the tea and cut a cake. "I know," she said.

"Do you like Rammy?"

"Yes. I have known him for such a long time. He often came to tea, sitting in the same place where you are sitting now. He had a heavy load to carry, I hope they'll treat him well in the mental home. He was frightened of people, you know, and very sorry that he left the sea. He often talked about his captain in Curaçao, a drunken old man I believe, but more of a father to him than his own."

"His father was married already," de Gier said.

"Yes. These things happen. But it's terrible for the children. They are lost and the world is empty to them."

A cat had come into the kitchen, it looked at Mrs. Buisman and purred. She picked it up and stroked its back.

"All living beings need love. This one too. I have to pick him up twenty times a day and tell him he is not alone."

"My cat," de Gier said, and jumped off his chair. "I must phone. Do you mind if I use your phone?"

"How is he?" Mrs. Buisman asked when de Gier had put the phone down.

"He's fine. My neighbor looks after him when I am out of town but my cat is a strange animal. He won't eat much when I am not there and he attacks whoever tries to get into the house. My neighbor doesn't mind, he is used to animals, he works in the zoo and he can handle Oliver. That's his name, Oliver. The neighbor is kind to him and Oliver can't defend himself against kindness."

"You see," Mrs. Buisman said. "Rammy is like that. He wants kindness but he has an aggressive way of asking for it."

De Gier stirred his tea. "Do you know Mr. Drachtsma, Mrs. Buisman?" he asked.

Mrs. Buisman narrowed her eyes. "I do."

"Did Rammy know him?"

"Rammy knew him well."

"What do you think of Mr. Drachtsma?"

Mrs. Buisman didn't look so pleasant now. Her face had become determined and her skin seemed tighter. De Gier suddenly noticed the stiff little bun on her head.

"You can tell me," de Gier said gently, "it's not mere curiosity."

"You've got your murderer, haven't you?" Mrs. Buisman asked.

De Gier began to eat his cake. "So it seems," he said with his mouth full.

"I have been thinking," Mrs. Buisman said. "Did Mr. Drachtsma know that murdered woman in Amsterdam?"

"Yes. She was his girlfriend, his mistress."

"Poor Mrs. Drachtsma."

"Didn't she know that her husband wasn't faithful?"

"Oh yes," Mrs. Buisman said gruffly, "she knew. She comes to tea here as well sometimes and she talked to me about it. She was trying to understand, she said. Important men travel about a lot and they have a lot of energy. One woman isn't enough for them. She said she didn't really mind as long as he wouldn't take his girlfriends to the island."

"Did he ever do that?"

"Perhaps. He often took people on his yacht. His wife never goes on the yacht, she is frightened of the sea."

"Yes, yes," de Gier said.

"He is not a nice man," Mrs. Buisman said after she had breathed deeply.

"Why not?"

Mrs. Buisman poured more tea and they were looking at each other, each stirring their tea mechanically.

"He used to remind me of a tumbleweed. You are a city man, aren't you, sergeant? You don't know about tumbleweeds?"

"I know a little about birds."

Mrs. Buisman laughed. "Yes, my husband told me about your adventure this morning."

"Oh, but I did enjoy it," de Gier said quickly, "but the adjutant, Grijpstra I mean, didn't feel well and we had the murder on our minds, of course."

"Never mind. I'll tell you about tumbleweeds. When the plants die here, at the end of the year, some of them break off. First they dry out and become brittle and one day the wind grabs them and they break their stems and begin to tumble all about the island. It's an amazing sight. The weeds seem so busy and so energetic, they go everywhere and when the wind changes they come back again. They bounce across the roads and get stuck against our fences, they even get into the gardens. The dunes are alive with them but eventually they will reach the beaches and then they drown in the sea, but they are dead already of course, they died long before they broke off and lost their souls.''

De Gier had put his cup down and was staring at the fat woman.

''Yes?'' he asked. ''Do you think Drachtsma lost his soul?''

''Soul, soul,'' Mrs. Buisman said. ''I am not a very Christian woman. I don't know about souls, it's just a manner of speaking. But Mr. Drachtsma is a hard man, he always gets his way, he bounces around and he never seems happy. Every year he buys a bigger boat and his cars never last and there are always carpenters and bricklayers working on his house. He is an unhappy man and he isn't really alive.''

''Who is alive?'' de Gier asked.

''Oh, lots of people are. My husband is. He is a loving man.''

De Gier smiled.

''Oh, not that way,'' Mrs. Buisman said and giggled. ''We aren't as young as we used to be. I mean he loves living things, and dead things too. The other day I saw him standing on the dike, looking at the sea and the birds and the clouds and I walked up to him and said 'Buisman' and he looked at me as if he didn't know who he was, he was so full of everything around him. But Drachtsma isn't like that, he always knows who he is. 'Drachtsma' is the most important word he knows and he is always thinking of how to make it bigger. And he'll be blown about by his endless desires the way the tumbleweeds are blown about by the wind.''

''And eventually he'll be blown into the sea and disappear,'' de Gier said.

Mrs. Buisman went to look after her patients and she

was away for a while. De Gier telephoned the hotel and was told to meet the commissaris at seven o'clock. He still had half an hour.

"Tell me, Mrs. Buisman," he said when she had come back again, smiling about something, "what was the relationship between Mr. Drachtsma and Rammy Scheffer?"

"I was thinking about that," Mrs. Buisman said, "but I forgot when I saw my two fat babies. Your Mr. Grijpstra certainly has a loud snore and my Buisman was wheezing right through it. I can't understand why they don't wake each other up. Rammy Scheffer, you say. Well, in the beginning, they just knew each other. Everybody knows everybody on the island, but I noticed that they had become closer, about a year ago it started, I think. Drachtsma always pretends he is interested in nature and he has donated a lot of money to the reserves. I know that he does care about the island; it's his home after all, his father came from the island, and his grandfather was born here, but I don't think Mr. Drachtsma cares about the birds. If he could build a hotel here he would probably do it but nobody is allowed to build hotels here anymore. I think Rammy went to see him about new fencing or something and after that they were sometimes together. I thought it was strange for they are so different. Rammy gets away from people, he'll work in his garden in his free time, and he sits near his fireplace and reads the Bible and Drachtsma always has people around him."

Mrs. Buisman began to play with her spoon.

"You don't know what they talked about?"

"I did overhear something of a conversation they were having," Mrs. Buisman said. "I was in the garden and they came past, I don't think they noticed me. Mr. Drachtsma was talking about 'evil' and Rammy was listening. 'Evil has to be destroyed, Rammy,' he was saying, and he said it again, and Rammy was listening very carefully."

"Thank you very much, Mrs. Buisman," de Gier said. "I'll have to go back to the commissaris. We are having dinner at Mr. Drachtsma's house tonight."

"Come again," Mrs. Buisman said, and opened the door for de Gier.

"I am not as silly as I look, sergeant," she said. "I know what you are after, but I don't think you have a chance. Nobody has ever been able to catch Mr. Drachtsma at anything."

De Gier smiled and thanked her for the tea.

"Not so fast," the commissaris said as they were walking toward the Drachtsma mansion. "My legs are about half the size of yours. And tell me the whole story again. Mrs. Buisman interests me, I should have come with you."

De Gier told the story again.

"Tumbleweeds," the commissaris said as they reached the gate and saw their host coming toward them. "I have heard about tumbleweeds before. Interesting, very."

19

In spite of the excellent food and the expensive wines which had poured from dusty bottles, de Gier hadn't enjoyed his meal. He had been placed opposite Mrs. Drachtsma, and the hard expression of her face, the thin lips, and the heavy coat of paint which almost cracked as she tried to look pleasant, had interfered with his digestion and he now felt as if his stomach were full of sand.

The interior of the house, contrary to his expectations, was dull. The house showed that its owner was rich, everything was of the best possible quality, but no imagination had been used and the heavy furniture stood where it should stand, heavily immobile, like trucks parked in a factory's courtyard. "Solid," de Gier was thinking, "just like my stomach. I couldn't even belch if I wanted to, there is no air."

They had been directed toward the fireplace and Drachtsma was pouring brandy. The commissaris was holding on to an enormous cigar and de Gier had rolled himself a cigarette from a little bag of tobacco which he had found in the pocket of his duffelcoat. He normally didn't roll his own cigarettes but he did it now as a feeble protest against the unsympathetic environment he had been forced into, and he had, almost rudely, refused the cigar which Drachtsma had offered.

"I have been to this island before," the commissaris was saying when he had finally managed to find a way of handling his cigar, "but in autumn, late autumn."

"That's a good time too," the mayor said. "The island is lovely in all seasons but I like it best just before winter. The tourists have gone by then and we have Schiermonnikoog to ourselves. It's a good time to walk on the beaches."

"That's what I was doing. I was very impressed by many things that evening. There was a strange atmosphere around me. Nature had died and the trees were bare and the seagulls were circling and yelling raucously and some crows were following me. Whenever I moved they would fly ahead and sit on a rock and stare at me. Crows are intelligent birds and they were talking to each other with their hoarse voices."

There was something about the way the commissaris was talking that wouldn't allow for interruptions and everybody was listening. Drachtsma had put the bottle down and was leaning against the mantelpiece, his long legs crossed and his hands in his pockets, but he didn't look casual.

"And then I saw the tumbleweed. I was on a wide stretch of beach, very wide perhaps, and I had walked close to the sea and I saw the tumbleweed coming down the dunes, rolling, being pushed by the wind. It was very big, perhaps ten feet across, and it wasn't just one dead plant, but I didn't know that at the time. I knew about tumbleweeds and I know that some of them do their trick on purpose. They grow special roots, late in their life, but the roots do not go into the ground. They touch the ground but they won't go in and yet they'll keep on growing. They are like arms which the weed uses to push itself up when the time comes. It starts pushing, using its long strong arms, and it pushes itself until it breaks away from its own proper roots and then it is free and begins to roll when the wind grabs it, and as it rolls it will meet other dead balls of branches and it will hook on to them and it goes on meeting others and they all tangle up together and finally the plants form one gigantic growth. I was seeing one of those that evening and it was coming straight for me. I ran to the left, but it changed direction, and then I ran to the right and it changed direction again. It was bouncing off the ground and twirling its yellow tentacles and it got me and pushed me into the sea, wanting to drown me." The commissaris' cigar had gone out and he busied himself with it.

"You are still alive," Drachtsma said, "so it failed, fortunately."

"It didn't mean to fail," the commissaris said, "and it gave me a good fright. I have never forgotten it. I have often thought of it since. What fascinates me is that I was being attacked by a corpse, by a thing without a will of its own. The plant had planned it all, but it had done so when it was still alive, and it had used its own dead body and the bodies of others to construct a weapon."

"Now, now," the mayor was saying, sipping his brandy and smiling. "It's a good story, of course, and I am sure it happened just the way you say it happened but you are exaggerating, I think. The plant never planned anything at all. It was a natural thing to happen. The dead plants tumble about to spread their seed. It happens after they have died, and it's extraordinary, and I agree that it is a fantastic sight to see them tumbling about on the beaches and through the dunes, but there is no evil in them."

The topic was changed and coffee was served and the conversation drifted this way and that for another hour and a half until the mayor and the aldermen got up and thanked the hostess for her hospitality. The commissaris and de

Gier had got up as well but Drachtsma offered them a final drink and Mrs. Drachtsma excused herself when he poured it and went to bed. The three men were standing near the fireplace, sipping the strong brandy.

"I liked your tumbleweed story," Drachtsma said, and the two policemen waited for him to continue but that was all Drachtsma was prepared to say.

"One entity killing another by using a third," the commissaris said.

"The tumbleweed using its own dead body to kill a living body," Drachtsma said.

"And the bodies of others," the commissaris said. "It is a good example of thought power. Businessmen often use it. They use others to achieve their purposes. They sit down and they keep on thinking in a certain direction and gradually a power builds up and finds an opportunity, a vehicle . . ."

De Gier put his glass down. "And Maria van Buren dies," he said. "Good night, Mr. Drachtsma. Thank you for a pleasant evening."

"I think *you* should have said that," Drachtsma said to the commissaris.

The commissaris shook Drachtsma's hand.

"Here is my card, Mr. Drachtsma. It has a telephone number on it."

Drachtsma was looking at his two visitors. "No," he said, "you don't *really* think that I will contact you, do you?"

20

Six months later, after the brains and memories of the policemen who had dealt with the Maria van Buren case had been soaked by a great many incidents relating to a number of other cases, the commissaris' telephone rang.

"Drachtsma," a faint voice said. "Do you remember me?"

The commissaris needed a few seconds.

"Yes, Mr. Drachtsma," he said. "I remember you."

"I would like to make a statement," the weak voice continued. It was speaking slowly, and carefully. "I would be grateful if you could come and visit me."

"Yes," the commissaris said, "but where are you?"

"On the island," Drachtsma said.

"Can't we put it off until you are in Amsterdam again?" the commissaris asked. "It's a bit of a trip from here to Schiermonnikoog and we are rather busy here. I believe you are often in Amsterdam, aren't you?"

"Not any more," the low voice said. "I am ill, very ill. I haven't left the island for months."

The commissaris looked at his window. The rain was
hitting it with such force that he couldn't see through it.

"What time is the next ferry?"

"If you leave your office now you'll arrive in time, and
you can go back on the afternoon ferry. You'll lose a day
but you'll be doing me an invaluable service."

"All right," the commissaris said.

"Pity Grijpstra didn't want to come," de Gier said.

Their car had crossed the Utrecht bridge and was joining
the main traffic on the speedway.

"You can't blame him," the commissaris said. "Nature almost got him last time and I think he must know the
island by now. Mrs. Buisman kept him for a full month,
didn't she?"

"She did," de Gier said. "Never in my life have I done
as much overtime as during that month."

"Be grateful," the commissaris said.

"Sir," said de Gier, who didn't understand.

Mrs. Drachtsma opened the door. Her face hadn't been
made up and she looked old and tired but some human
warmth seemed to radiate from her being.

"I am so glad you could come," she said. "My husband is waiting for you. He has cancer of the lungs and the
doctor thinks he is getting close to the end. He didn't want
to go to the hospital on the mainland, and he refused the
ray treatment they were recommending. He kept on saying
that the rays could only lengthen the torture."

"How long has your husband been ill, madam?" the
commissaris asked.

"The cancer was diagnosed three months ago. He is
very weak now."

IJsbrand Drachtsma had been put into a large metal
hospital bed. Three pillows kept his head and shoulders
upright. His face was the color of ivory and his eyes had

sunk deeply under the thin dry bristles of his eyebrows. The commissaris and de Gier touched the white hand on which veins crinkled like blue worms.

Drachtsma coughed and wheezed with every breath. He was trying to speak. "Tumbleweed," he said after a while, coughing at every syllable. "You remember?"

"Yes," the commissaris said, "but don't strain yourself, Drachtsma. I think I can understand you without you trying to talk. If talking hurts you we don't want you to talk. We'll stay here awhile if you like, we'll just sit here in the room, and maybe we'll ask a few questions and you can nod your head or shake it."

Drachtsma smiled. "No. I've got to talk. You were right, it happened the way you said it happened."

The commissaris wanted to stop him but Mrs. Drachtsma put a hand on his shoulder.

"Please let him talk, commissaris. I know what he wants to say. He has told me and I have forgiven him. I have even understood him. But he wants to tell you. Let him tell you, it will give him peace."

"Yes," Drachtsma said. "I would like Rammy to be here but my wife phoned the clinic and he is still ill. My fault. I used him instead of trying to help him. I could have helped him but I didn't know it at the time, didn't want to know. Too late now. Pity."

He began to cough again and Mrs. Drachtsma cradled his shoulders in her arm and he put his face on her neck.

De Gier felt suffocated, he wanted to get up and leave the room and smoke in the corridor but the quietness of the commissaris next to him helped him to restrain himself.

"It's all right," said Drachtsma, and smiled at his wife. "Childish, that's the word. I have always been childish. Not this, to be embraced by your wife isn't childish. But what I have been doing all my life was silly. Always choose my own benefit, what I thought was my own benefit. Maria was my toy, I didn't want her to have a life of her own. She could have other men, but her attachment had to be to me. And I didn't want her to be a witch."

"A witch," de Gier muttered.

"Yes, she was a good witch."

"Good?" the commissaris asked.

"A good bad witch. Efficient. Knew her job. The herbs helped but they were only part of it. She had learned and practiced and experimented. A dedicated woman. Things like that don't come easy, you know. A lot of trips to Curaçao and she didn't enjoy going there anymore, not with her family all against her. But it got her somewhere. I don't know where. It gave her power. She could pull people. Me too. Anytime she wanted me to come I came, like a doll on a string."

"So you killed her?" the commissaris asked.

Drachtsma nodded.

His wife poured a cup of tea and helped him to take a sip.

"Yes. I had her killed. I was too clever to do it myself. I thought of it but you would have connected me with her death. I know how to make other people work for me, how to use people. I picked her own brother. I thought that was very clever. I was proud of my intelligence. I have always been proud. Pride is good sometimes, it helped me get away during the war. But it is dangerous too. Pride should be a tool, a man should be in charge of his own pride."

Drachtsma closed his eyes.

"Rammy," he said suddenly. "Rammy was my tool. I willed him into throwing that knife. I gave him the knife. It was my own knife. I had kept it in a box, nobody knew I had it. I worked on Rammy for a long time, told him his sister was evil. A whore. A witch. He had to kill her. To keep the world clean. He knew where she lived, he had been there once, a long time ago. He hated her, he was jealous of her. She was a real child of his father, he wasn't. Jealousy makes people very easy to handle."

"My wife forgave me," Drachtsma said. "Do you forgive me, commissaris?"

"Yes," the commissaris said.

"There are others, too many others. Rammy is one of them. I can't ask them. And there is no other chance, I would like to have another chance."

Drachtsma drank more tea.

"Shon Wancho," the commissaris said.

Drachtsma's eyes opened again.

"The witch doctor," Drachtsma said. "Yes."

"Did you know him?"

Drachtsma shook his head. "No. I never went to Curaçao. I didn't want to go and I don't think she wanted me to either."

"What do you think? Is he an evil man?"

Drachtsma shook his head. "No. Not evil."

"A good man?"

"Yes," Drachtsma said. "He warned her. She told me he warned her. She talked about him in her sleep."

"So what did she learn from Shon Wancho?" the commissaris asked.

"Insight," Drachtsma said and coughed. "Just insight."

"And *she* had to find out what to do with it?"

"Yes. Magical insight. Strong. Can be used the wrong way. She did."

"What happens if you use it the wrong way?" de Gier asked. He couldn't help asking it. He would have preferred to sit quietly, waiting for the ordeal to be over.

"If you use it wrong," Drachtsma said slowly, "you go wrong."

There seemed nothing else to say and the commissaris looked at Mrs. Drachtsma and pointed at the door with his head.

"Yes, commissaris," Mrs. Drachtsma said.

De Gier was at the door when Drachtsma called him. He walked back and bowed down to the slack body in the large bed. The white hand came up slowly and closed on de Gier's wrist.

"Don't win," Drachtsma said. "To try to win is child-ish."

De Gier wanted to go but the hand held his wrist.

"Sergeant," Drachtsma whispered.

"Yes, Mr. Drachtsma."

"Don't ever try to win. You are still young. You can unlearn a lot."

"Yes, Mr. Drachtsma," de Gier said.

Curtain

HERCULE POIROT'S LAST AND GREATEST CASE

Agatha Christie

_____ 80720 CURTAIN $1.95

Available at bookstores everywhere, or order direct from the publisher.